D1473058

Ardenia Dovie's

Card Catalog

Franni!
Dance! Dream! Delight!

JAN HUNEYCUTT LIGHTNER

Jan
3-18-2017

Permissions
Grateful acknowledgment is made to Darlene Fuller, granddaughter of Verona Elizabeth Wagner Lyden, for granting permission to reprint previously published lyrics to *Christ Ambassadors*. Words and melody by Mrs. George Wagner © 1928.

ISBN-13: 978-1535283083
ISBN-10: 1535283084

For every Ardenia Dovie,
every age, gender, and circumstance, stories told or not.
May you be free from pain and suffering. May you be free from
fear and anxiety. May you be happy. May you be
at peace.

Deepest bows to all who open eyes, ears, minds, and hearts
to those with the hardest stories. Peace to you, too.

And, a little curtsy to Janet, who always wanted to write a book,
and did.

Acknowledgements

Mitch Lightner, Sara Huneycutt, and Jesse Huneycutt, saying thanks to you hardly counts. But I'm saying it anyway. *Thank you.* You three have been supportive in more ways than I can mention here. I don't claim to know much but here's one thing I do know: No matter what life offers or brings *or throws at* me, you, you, you are my ground.

Baxter Bittle, Gibson Bittle, Amis Johnson, Izzy Huneycutt, and Kaylee Cofield, if in the future you read this story, let's talk. Say, let's talk anyway. About anything at all. I'm always ready. Because of you, my grandsons, my granddaughters, my world overflows with curiosity, inspiration, joy, hope, and laughter. Brielle Thompson, we are closer than ever before, but, oh, my heart will always ache.

Diana Rogers, Donna Fallin, Julia Melson, Leah Floyd Dillard, Marisa Nabholz, Martha Dewing, Missy Reed, Nan Schoonover, Pan Adams-McCaslin, and Sandy Wright, most of you read every single card! Sometimes, more than once. I'm beyond grateful for your questions, responses, suggestions, and opinions. I didn't always take your advice (surprise!) but you compelled me to pause and reconsider. Your encouragement strengthened my resolve to share this tale. Sara, my daughter, when I got stuck, most often it was you who knew what I needed. Ali'a Brooke, Amy Grau, Joanie Barrett Roberts, Linda Park-Fuller, Liz Wagner, and Terry Hanson, your cheering was constant. And it was music to my ears. Edie Skalitzky, you just never tire of joyfully envisioning with me new expressions of love. Yes! And, kudos to Aron Shelton for creating an online home for Ardenia Dovie. Thank you all for believing.

It's been said that the roots of the tree reveal the fruit of the tree. My siblings, we share a deep and marvelous root system, don't we? Hopefully, the fruit I bear is the loving fruit I see in you.

Speaking of roots, everything I am, everything I do, and every story I tell, somehow has its beginnings with my parents, Darrel Walker Rogers and Linda Carolyn Pugh Rogers. My gratitude for having had them as my parents is simply inexpressible. I have no doubt, if given the chance to hold this book in their hands, each would shake their head at some of the language. (Sorry, Mom and Dad. Ardenia Dovie made me do it. She *insisted*.) I like to think, though, they would also smile, at least occasionally, and experience the sweet return of some old shared memories. Even now, in death, Daddy still "sings his way into my heart" and Mama still says, "Tell me."

Above all, below all, and through it all, I thank the One I know as Mystery.

Ardenia Dovie's
Card Catalog

Date: Monday, December 31, 1973

Topic: Card Catalog

Category: Thing

Author: Ardenia Dovie Carroll

Location: 727 Rt. 323, Penny Pass, AR

A card catalog is a collection of cards all the same size, arranged in a logical order, like in the library. Each card gives information on one thing. This is my alternative to a diary or journal - a way to capture and <u>organize</u> my thoughts and feelings, maybe even my life! I'll have to be careful about what I write because these cards are only four inches wide by six inches high. This means I've got 12 lines for writing. My seven categories will be: People, Places, Things, Feelings, Poetry, Music, and Actions. I can change these after I get started and I can give cards more than just one category.

January
1974

Date: Tuesday, January 1, 1974

Topic: Ardenia Dovie Carroll

Category: People

Author: Ardenia Dovie Carroll

Location: 727 Rt. 323, Penny Pass, AR

Ardenia: think Gardenia without the G. Dovie: think of the morning dove and add an i before the e. Carroll: just remember 2 r's and 2 l's. I'm 12 years old. A straight 'A' student in 7th grade at Skiddy, AR. I live in the only parsonage in Penny Pass, population 240. I'm daughter to Collie Cade and Ruby Carroll. Dilly-Dally (Dilly), a tri-colored beagle, is my dog. I'm a born again Christian. I read the Bible almost every day but here's the truth: I don't really like to. I prefer novels. I might want to be a writer or poet someday. Or a teacher. I like God's great outdoors. I pray without ceasing.

Date: Wednesday, January 2, 1974

Topic: Collie Cade Carroll

Category: People

Author: Ardenia Dovie Carroll

Location: 727 Rt. 323, Penny Pass, AR

First, he's my daddy. He's a good preacher and he pastors the only church in Penny Pass. The church sign (which I help change each week) right now says, "If your life stinks, we've got a pew for you." He isn't always, but he <u>can</u> be funny. Daddy knows all about winning souls for Christ and fixing cars. Both come in handy. He's an expert (and very loud!) whistler. Before the Lord saved him, he liked his alcohol and cigarettes. When I was a baby, he gave his heart to Jesus, and he was delivered from both. Now, he likes to pray and study the Bible. He sings a lot, too.

Date: Wednesday, January 2, 1974

Topic: Ruby Jane Carroll

Category: People

Author: Ardenia Dovie Carroll

Location: 727 Rt. 323, Penny Pass, AR

My mom's very first name was Ruby Jane Evans. She was born in California and Daddy teases her sometimes about what she doesn't know about living in the country. She's a trooper, though. She puts up with him! She's a Christian, but she's a quiet one. About the only time she talks about God is when she's teaching Sunday School to the little kids or when she's telling someone she'll pray for them. She <u>loves</u> to read. She reads whatever I bring home from my school library. Sometimes I get extra books that I think she'll like. She hums while she works. (Daddy whistles, Mama hums a lot.)

Date: Thursday, January 3, 1974

Topic: Fuck

Category: ?

Author: Ardenia Dovie Carroll

Location: 727 Rt. 323, Penny Pass, AR

Fuck is still a complete mystery to me. I can't even categorize it! All I know is it's a bad word. I think it has to do with nakedness and sin because the word sort of feels like when Daddy preaches about fornication or Sodom and Gomorrah. When he barks about keeping bodies covered, I feel uncomfortable in my skin. I begin to fidget and can't look him or anyone else in the eye. Fuck probably takes you straight to hell. Shouldn't I know what it is then? I finally spelled it, quickly, to ask Mom, but she wouldn't say. She shook her head a few times and frowned. And, she'll probably tell Dad.

Date: Friday, January 4, 1974

Topic: Tyrone Shepley Dobbs

Category: People

Author: Ardenia Dovie Carroll

Location: 727 Rt. 323, Penny Pass, AR

Shep lives across the street. He's 11 and has a little brother. His family goes to our church. Mama says he's a nice boy. He and I ride the bus together and look out for each other. We like riding bikes, and being daring on them. Sometimes we ride over to Clarks for candy or ice cream or a bottle of pop. Shep might be my best friend. But he is a boy. His straight blond hair hangs in his eyes. When he's sweaty, it sticks to his face and he kind of has a big nose. Once Dad referred to him as Sheepdog. Mama gasped, "Collie!" Then added, "And with a name like yours?" and Dad mumbled, "Sorry."

Date: Saturday, January 5, 1974

Topic: DST - Daylight Savings Time

Category: Thing

Author: Ardenia Dovie Carroll

Location: 727 Rt. 323, Penny Pass, AR

Oil prices have tripled in the last 5 months, so Daylight Savings will begin 4 months early. I guess this is big news. Yesterday in Social Studies, Mr. Mabry said that in World War II Pres. Roosevelt set up DST in Feb 1942 and it lasted 3½ years. Now Congress wants to keep this DST through April 1975. Somehow this will save 200,000 barrels of fuel per day. I do not know how because, regardless of where the hour hands on the clock are, you use electricity when it's dark. You can see no better in the morning dark than the night dark. We should just stick with one time or the other.

Date: Sunday, January 6, 1974

Topic: The Olive Branch Assembly of God Church

Category: Place, People

Author: Ardenia Dovie Carroll

Location: 727 Rt. 323, Penny Pass, AR

Established in 1919, Olive Branch has 87 members. On Sun mornings, attendance is 63 to 111. More people come on Sun morning than on Sun or Wed nights, but the singing's <u>always</u> better on Sun night. Wed night is calmer; Daddy teaches rather than preaches. Outside, our rock walls rise tabby-cat colored. Inside, pews and pulpit are as dark as walnuts. Hymnals, scab red. A white bell tower pokes out of the roof; a long white rope drops down through a small hole to where we meet and greet. I toll the bell at 9 a.m. on Sun mornings and on New Year's Eve. Sometimes it's hard to stop!

Date: Monday, January 7, 1974

Topic: Love

Category: Action, Feeling

Author: Ardenia Dovie Carroll

Location: 727 Rt. 323, Penny Pass, AR

Love is putting others first: God, then others,
last yourself. 1st Cor. 13 explains: Patient. Kind.
Beareth, believeth, hopeth, and endureth all things.
Putting others' needs and I guess their wants
before your own. Ultimate love is laying down
your very life (dying) for someone. Sacrificing even
yourself. Which is what Jesus did. Which to me is
much more loving than sacrificing someone else!
How could it be love when God told Abraham to
sacrifice his own child? Is obedience greater than
love? Is it ever the same thing? How does someone
know?

Date: Tuesday, January 8, 1974

Topic: Card Catalog Organization

Category: Action, Thing

Author: Ardenia Dovie Carroll

Location: 727 Rt. 323, Penny Pass, AR

There are five ways I could organize these cards. Author, which makes no sense because I'm the only one writing! Location could be interesting. What I write where. Topic would be a real headache. Category? Date? By date sure would be easier. I'll just write and drop them in the box. Maybe I'll get some monthly dividers. Maybe at the end of the year, I'll re-sort by Category. Just for fun. Look at all of my People cards all together. All of my Actions. Places, Things, and so on. I could find out what was the biggest category. And what was the smallest. I wonder what else I'll learn.

Date: Wednesday, January 9, 1974

Topic: Female Attire

Category: Thing

Author: Ardenia Dovie Carroll

Location: 727 Rt. 323, Penny Pass, AR

There are more rules for girls so boys have it easy. Dad didn't let Mom or me wear pants (or shorts, sleeveless tops, or swimsuits) until I began 6th grade and PE was mandatory. I was afraid he'd suggest I just safety pin my dress between my legs (like women do for baptisms or swimming) before jumping jacks or sit ups. Luckily, he didn't. When others changed from pants to shorts, I swapped my dress for pants. Now, I wear pants everywhere but to church. (Still no PE shorts.) I'm not sure what changed but he says pants help cover our bodies. Fine by me, I love pants.

Date: Thursday, January 10, 1974

Topic: My Room

Category: Place

Author: Ardenia Dovie Carroll

Location: 727 Rt. 323, Penny Pass, AR

My room is painted July early morning blue. The furniture: buckeye brown. On my nightstand: an AM/FM radio but I only play FM. Every night. On my dresser: a record player, 3 records (Bread, Jim Croce, the Carpenters), my little-girl jewelry box (holding special rocks and my birthstone ring which is diamond and looks like a promise ring), my white zippered Bible (my name in gold), and a pint jar of colored pencils, sharp points up. A scraggly Wandering Jew falls from my macramé hanger nearly to the floor. On one wall: The Good Shepherd with 1 black sheep squeezing in, nearly hiding behind Him.

Date: Friday, January 11, 1974

Topic: Penis

Category: Thing

Author: Ardenia Dovie Carroll

Location: 727 Rt. 323, Penny Pass, AR

A penis is a boy's private part. It's usually soft.
When you change a baby boy's diaper and need to
clean him up, you have to move it around carefully but confidently. Don't be scared. But, be respectful. Pee comes out of the very end. It can
get hard and bigger. Pee can come out when it's
soft or hard. It probably gets bigger as the baby
grows, just like noses do. In T.V. movies, when the
man pees, you just see his back but he's doing
something with his hands. Maybe if they don't hold
it, it whirls around. Like a hose. I've heard Mama
tell Daddy to do a better job of aiming.

Date: Saturday, January 12, 1974

Topic: Who is this?

Category: Poetry - Intentional

Author: Ardenia Dovie Carroll

Location: 727 Rt. 323, Penny Pass, AR

No two snowflakes just alike
No two thumbprints just alike
Each little pig had his own sense of home
Each bear, their favorite bed
Seven dwarfs,
seven tools,
seven names,
and moods
Who is this girl that writes
these words?

Date: Sunday, January 13, 1974

Topic: The Rapture

Category: Thing, Action

Author: Ardenia Dovie Carroll

Location: 727 Rt. 323, Penny Pass, AR

Also known as the Second Coming of Jesus. It's like an emergency exit plan. It'll happen when it looks like the world can't get any worse. (Afterwards, it will!) We have to stay ready. Instead of packing a suitcase, we keep our hearts white as snow. Which we can't do on our own. It's where Jesus comes in. Our part is asking forgiveness for all our wrongs. Then, when we least expect it, a trumpet will sound, (like the tornado siren), Jesus will part the heavens (like a curtain), and believers, alive and dead, will rise to meet Him in the clouds. Fear of heights, gone. Just like that.

Date: Monday, January 14, 1974

Topic: Accidental Poetry

Category: Thing, Action

Author: Ardenia Dovie Carroll

Location: 727 Rt. 323, Penny Pass, AR

Accidental poetry is written by randomly opening books, magazines, newspapers, or the Bible and letting your fingers or your eyes pick phrases. To get started, without cheating, point to some words. Write them down. Then, just flip through and skim for the rest of the lines. If you aren't a little picky while skimming, it won't make any sense at all. You can place a whole phrase on a line, or you can break it up however you want. Your limit is 12 lines. I'll write one accidental poem right now. From Mom's Good Housekeeping.

Date: Monday, January 14, 1974

Topic: Failure

Category: Poetry - Accidental

Author: Ardenia Dovie Carroll

Location: 727 Rt. 323, Penny Pass, AR

Failure.
What went wrong?
Welcome
to
looking back.
Don't trust anyone
else's;
Your
inside return
is a
wake-up
to strength.

Date: Tuesday, January 15, 1974

Topic: Pants

Category: Thing

Author: Ardenia Dovie Carroll

Location: 727 Rt. 323, Penny Pass, AR

I love pants. Why? Well, 1) I like the way they hold my bottom. 2) They make my legs look longer. 3) I don't have to sit with my knees together! 4) They are much warmer in winter. Mom and I weren't allowed to wear them until last year. Now that we can, she's made me polyester pants with side zippers in pine green, robin egg blue, burnt sienna / cream plaid, black hounds tooth, and plum. With my own money, I bought white bell bottom hip-hugger jeans. (If Dad's noticed any hip-hugging, he's not said.) Mom made herself pants in navy, camel, black, and charcoal. I think she likes wearing them, too.

Date: Wednesday, January 16, 1974

Topic: Skiddy School

Category: Place

Author: Ardenia Dovie Carroll

Location: 727 Rt. 323, Penny Pass, AR

Skiddy has 20-25 kids (one whole class) per grade. Most of the 6th through 12th-grade classes are in a big old 2-story building. The outside walls match Olive Branch's rock. Upstairs, well-worn wood floors ripple like waves and sink with our weight. The basement floor is concrete, painted gray, and chipped. Apple trees (3) flank the main sidewalk. The Principal has 2 Vice-Principals: one for us; one for the elementary school, which is one level, much newer, and on the other side of the playground. We arrive, mostly riding buses, from all over. I'm nice to everyone; but Shep is my closest friend.

Date: Thursday, January 17, 1974

Topic: Winter Slippers

Category: Thing

Author: Ardenia Dovie Carroll

Location: 727 Rt. 323, Penny Pass, AR

I get new slippers every Christmas. I've never wondered why before. I thought it was just a Christmas thing. But I guess it's because each winter my feet will barely fit, or won't fit at all, into my old ones. Mama and Daddy have had theirs for years. I'm so used to the old things, I haven't really been seeing them. Daddy's not only look uncomfortable, they are. I know. I trounced around in them when I was little. They're horseshoe heavy. Today, Mama took a needle and thread to hers. Mark my word, I'm buying them each a new pair next Christmas.

Date: Friday, January 18, 1974

Topic: Whacky Cake - needs no icing

Category: Thing

Author: Ardenia Dovie Carroll

Location: 727 Rt. 323, Penny Pass, AR

1 cup sugar	3 tbsp cocoa
½ tsp soda	1 cup cold water
½ tsp salt	1 tbsp vinegar
1 ½ cup flour	6 tbsp butter

Mix everything well and pour into ungreased oblong pan. Bake at 350° for about 25-30 minutes.

This is one of my favorites. Anytime Mom makes it, I end up eating little squares all day long so it only lasts a few days.

Date: Saturday, January 19, 1974

Topic: Dilly Dally

Category: People

Author: Ardenia Dovie Carroll

Location: 727 Rt. 323, Penny Pass, AR

Dilly arrived one year ago today. I say it was serendipitous. Dad says he came "special-delivery." As in dropped off. Dilly was outside, shaking. Of course, I asked to bring him in. Dad's answer? "No." But I couldn't sleep. At 11 pm, I got bold. Woke Daddy up to ask one more time. He sighed, got up, and let that cold puppy in. Dilly was exuberant. Daddy wrapped him in a towel. I mixed corn flakes and Cheerios; warmed some milk. Daddy said, "He can stay in your room, <u>not</u> in your bed" so I pulled my covers off and joined him on the floor. The next morning, Dad shook his head but smiled.

Date: Sunday, January 20, 1974

Topic: Impatience

Category: Feeling, Action

Author: Ardenia Dovie Carroll

Location: 727 Rt. 323, Penny Pass, AR

Mom has a particular way of showing impatience but you have to know what to look for. I've seen it my whole life. First, her left eye squints in just the slightest way, Then comes the slight double, sometimes triple, twitch. Lately, I've seen it at least three times a week. After every service, Sister Geneva has been going on and on and on about her aches and pains. If I'm standing to Mom's right, I see nothing. But if I'm on her left, I see the squint, and the twitch, and then her entire face suddenly smooths right out until not even I can tell.

Date: Monday, January 21, 1974

Topic: Saved

Category: Action, People

Author: Ardenia Dovie Carroll

Location: 727 Rt. 323, Penny Pass, AR

I got saved when I was six. I like to think that if I had died in a car crash before then, I'd have gone to heaven. Daddy says there's an age of accountability, but it can be different for different people. After that point, a person has to ask Jesus to be their personal Savior and to accept Him as such. Some churches baptize babies. Not us. It isn't up to the parents. They can <u>dedicate</u> their children like Samuel's mom, Hannah, did. In doing this, they promise to teach and train their children so that their hearts are primed to turn over to God. I was primed.

Date: Tuesday, January 22, 1974

Topic: Games

Category: Thing, Action, Feelings

Author: Ardenia Dovie Carroll

Location: 727 Rt. 323, Penny Pass, AR

I just now remembered playing London Bridge as a kid. Bending and trying to get through the arch two other kids made by holding hands and lifting them high. Being caught and rocked back and forth against bony forearms. Singing "take a key and lock her up, my fair lady." Some kids would just lob you back and forth while they had you locked up, while others were determined to render bruises. I was one of those kids that went easy on the captured. Why ever try to hurt someone on purpose? It's a game. Smiles going in, smiles coming out.

Date: Wednesday, January 23, 1974

Topic: Fishing

Category: Action

Author: Ardenia Dovie Carroll

Location: 727 Rt. 323, Penny Pass, AR

Fishing for men means saving souls for Christ. It means witnessing to people about how much God loves them (John 3:16) but if they don't give their hearts to Jesus most likely they'll spend eternity burning in hell. It's about the only time I can say "hell". Otherwise, it's cussing. The other kind of fishing -for shimmery fish- is easy in comparison. You hope something takes your bait but you don't worry about it. If you don't haul one in, you don't feel guilty. You squish a wriggling worm onto the hook, drop a line, and chill. 1, 2, 3, easy peasy.

Date: Thursday, January 24, 1974

Topic: Careers

Category: People

Author: Ardenia Dovie Carroll

Location: 727 Rt. 323, Penny Pass, AR

There're a lot of things I just don't want to be: a switchboard operator, a hairdresser, a dog groomer, a telephone lineman, a plumber, an electrician, a stay-at-home mom, a nurse. But, maybe a librarian. All of those <u>books</u>! Perhaps a teacher. For kids, say kindergarteners. I always want to write that last part with a "d". Kindergar<u>d</u>en. A kinder garden. I can imagine reading to them every day and encouraging them to count higher and higher, and learn those ABC's! And, we would have fun songs about everything. Imagine all that curiosity and all those big personalities in tiny little packages!

Date: Friday, January 25, 1974

Topic: Cheering

Category: Action

Author: Ardenia Dovie Carroll

Location: 727 Rt. 323, Penny Pass, AR

We're big, B-I-G, and we're bad, B-A-D, and we're boss B-O-S, B-O-S-S, boss. My favorite cheer. I'm not allowed to be a cheerleader. Even if I could, I wouldn't want to be. In front of everybody twirling around, yelling. Standing with fists on hips, back straight, waiting for the next cheer order. I'm not in the booster club either, which may be allowed because jeans are worn. But you have to stand and cheer on command, and stay put until halftime. I wear my maroon/white leopard t-shirt and white Levi's, sit wherever I want, root as I choose, and traipse to the concessions as needed.

Date: Saturday, January 26, 1974

Topic: Spatting

Category: Action

Author: Ardenia Dovie Carroll

Location: 727 Rt. 323, Penny Pass, AR

Mom and Dad have had a spat. They didn't talk all the way into town. He whistled a bit but the air in the car was still tight. He cracked the window. He rested his arm on the back of the seat and touched her shoulder but Mom shifted away. She just looked out the window. I couldn't decide between going into the beauty shop with her and running errands with him. When she got out, not looking at either of us, she said, "Ardenia. Just keep your dad company." He didn't even wait for me to get in the front seat before he took off. Their spats never last long, though.

Date: Saturday, January 26, 1974

Topic: Making Up

Category: Action

Author: Ardenia Dovie Carroll

Location: 727 Rt. 323, Penny Pass, AR

Daddy chewed his last bite, put his fork down on his plate, and said, "Ruby, we need to talk. Let's talk." (He preaches about not letting the sun go down on your anger. Especially in a marriage.) Mama sighed and said she knew that. I said, "I can go to my room. I'll just go right now." I didn't even take my plate to the sink. I should have closed my door but I stood in my doorway and listened. Their words were like tennis on TV, racquet against ball. Back and forth. Then their voices grew softer, slower. Like underhanded ball tossing and I knew they'd made up. Quietly, I shut my door.

Date: Sunday, January 27, 1974

Topic: This Catalog

Category: Thing

Author: Ardenia Dovie Carroll

Location: 727 Rt. 323, Penny Pass, AR

I bought four packages of 100 cards. Rather than doing one or a few at a time, I've decided to show my commitment by preparing the rest. I've written the headers, wrote my name as Author, and prepared one card per day. Plus some extras without dates. I used every spare minute this weekend. I told Mom and Dad I'm working on a project. A big one. They looked at each other and then nodded at me. When Mama said, "Ok, Honey. Just let us know if you need us to look it over," I said, "Nope, I have to do it all by myself. It's required." It felt like a white lie.

Date: Monday, January 28, 1974

Topic: Light - Matthew 5:15 and 16

Category: Action

Author: Ardenia Dovie Carroll

Location: 727 Rt. 323, Penny Pass, AR

I lit a candle in my room and watched. First, it flickered and sputtered. Finally it took hold and burned steady. In all directions, it gave out light. It didn't _decide_ where to shine. It just shone, offering light 360°. "Neither do men (meaning anyone) light a candle, and put it under a bushel, but on a candlestick; and it giveth light unto all that are in the house. Let your light so shine before men (meaning everyone) that they may see your good works, and glorify your Father which is in heaven." I want to be one of God's lights. All of the time. Everywhere. To everyone.

Date: Tuesday, January 29, 1974

Topic: My Closet

Category: Place

Author: Ardenia Dovie Carroll

Location: 727 Rt. 323, Penny Pass, AR

Organization helps save time and can keep you from getting frustrated. "A place for everything and everything in its place" isn't just a saying, so my dresses start on the right. Maxis, midis, then others. Next, skirts. Then, all tops. Then, pants. Three purses hang by straps on a nail in the back. In case I ever want to "grow up and be a lady." I do not see that happening anytime soon. Another nail: belts, which I try not to use. On the shelf above my head: two stacks of folded sweaters. Shoes are lumped on the floor. How hard can finding a pair of shoes be?

Date: Wednesday, January 30, 1974

Topic: Make a Joyful Noise

Category: Action

Author: Ardenia Dovie Carroll

Location: 727 Rt. 323, Penny Pass, AR

I've heard about churches that have no music. They sing songs without any accompaniment. Someone might just hum a note and everybody just takes off. At Olive Branch, we've got a piano, drums, acoustic and electric guitars, a bass, and a tambourine at almost every service. Sometimes a harmonica. Occasionally there'll be a saxophone or flute for a special song. Every so often, a teenager, who can't play anything else, will bring in their mom's spoons and, in the scope of one song, it will become apparent to everyone if the spoons are too much, too.

Date: Thursday, January 31, 1974

Topic: The Widowmaker

Category: Place

Author: Ardenia Dovie Carroll

Location: 727 Rt. 323, Penny Pass, AR

This is a hairpin curve between Penny Pass and Skiddy. Dad says it's so sharp your front end reaches round and kisses your rear end. It's an accident waiting to happen and almost everyone knows of someone who has died on one side of it or the other. Besides being sharp, the lean is off; it's hard to stay in your own yellow line. Two tiny white crosses have been pounded into the cold ground. Two teddy bears and two plastic wreathes startle one into silence. This curve makes widows and widowers out of wives and husbands. Not parents. What do you call them?

February

1974

Date: Friday, February 1, 1974

Topic: One Happy Cat

Category: Thing

Author: Ardenia Dovie Carroll

Location: 727 Rt. 323, Penny Pass, AR

Last night, at the bottom of a drawer I found my little old happy blue and white polka-dotted perfume cat pin from Avon. The screw-on cap was grimy in the grooves. The perfume smells about the same as I remember. Back then, I thought it was nifty having perfume so handy. But how handy does perfume need to be? How often does a kid need to put it on? How often did I? For fun, I pinned it on today and applied it every time I thought about it. By bath time, I'd dabbed 27 times. It was a happy little cat but I bet everyone else wasn't! And I have a Topaz headache.

Date: Saturday, February 2, 1974

Topic: Chores

Category: Thing

Author: Ardenia Dovie Carroll

Location: 727 Rt. 323, Penny Pass, AR

There are daily chores: make your bed, help with dishes, pick up after yourself. There are "every 2- or 3- day" chores: laundry, sweeping. Weekly chores: dust, scrub tub, clean the church. Seasonal chores: Spring cleaning, window washing. Summer gardening, getting fruits and vegetables into the freezer. Autumn leaf raking (though we're not so good at this), cutting and splitting wood. Winter pipe wrapping for insulation, vent closing in the crawlspace. Annual chores: turning the septic tank valve. Chores as needed: just doing what must be done.

Date: Sunday, February 3, 1974

Topic: My Period!

Category: Thing

Author: Ardenia Dovie Carroll

Location: 727 Rt. 323, Penny Pass, AR

I got it! I really am becoming a woman. I think it's called a "period" because it happens periodically. What's it like? Messy. Mama already had a slim white Wonderform belt for me. It has garter thingys you push the Kotex ends into. It's tricky. When I get it just right, the pad hugs me gently but firmly. The contraption feels funny, especially until I get my panties pulled up. Practice makes perfect, so I'll get better at it. Unluckily, my insides feel like they might fall right out. This crampiness is different than other tummy cramps. Mom says to keep foil-wrapped Midol in my locker.

Date: Monday, February 4, 1974

Topic: My Very First Period

Category: Thing, Action

Author: Ardenia Dovie Carroll

Location: 727 Rt. 323, Penny Pass, AR

Well, it's something all right. While I'm glad to be becoming a woman, I still have a lot to learn before I feel confident about what I'm doing. This trial and error period (ha! get it?) could have some very embarrassing moments. Mama helped me yesterday but now I just have to practice and figure things out on my own. The 7th grade booklets have come in handy. I'm glad I kept them. Going to school was weirder than being at church. It's one thing to sit straight down on a pew, it's another thing altogether to slide into those desk-chairs.

Date: Tuesday, February 5, 1974

Topic: Bodies

Category: Things

Author: Ardenia Dovie Carroll

Location: 727 Rt. 323, Penny Pass, AR

Our bodies are fearfully and wonderfully made.
They were more wonderful before Eve and Adam
sinned, bringing about all of those consequences.
Now we might consider them to be more fearfully
made. Sometimes I feel like my body and I are the
same but this is problematic. The body is sinful;
the flesh is weak. To relate to my body too much
might be asking for trouble. On one hand, we're
trying to figure them out. Take care of them.
Keep them in line. On the other, we're trying not
to identify with them. It seems to be a never-
ending battle.

Date: Wednesday, February 6, 1974

Topic: Books

Category: Thing

Author: Ardenia Dovie Carroll

Location: 727 Rt. 323, Penny Pass, AR

I know we shouldn't have false idols. But I swear (if I could) I feel like dropping to my knees when I'm around a lot of books. I love them and how they're filled with words that start with only 26 letters! In study hall, there's a long, long, long wall of books. I always sit next to them and, when I enter or exit or have to walk around the room, I run my hands along their colored spines. The noise that makes comforts me like lullabies used to. Sometimes, I look for the book that's sticking out the most. If one reaches for me, I reach right back. It's one I'll have to borrow.

Date: Thursday, February 7, 1974

Topic: Kidnapping

Category: Action

Author: Ardenia Dovie Carroll

Location: 727 Rt. 323, Penny Pass, AR

Patty Hearst, the 19-yr-old daughter of a million-aire, was kidnapped. The kidnappers told her rich family to give $70 dollars of food for every poor person who lives in CA. How can they figure out how many there are? Where should the food be taken? How do you give it out? For some reason, Mr. Hearst chose the Bay Area, and donated $2 million to go for food there. He had to do some-thing. He wanted his girl back. Then the kidnappers decided they wanted another $4 million and now they won't let her go. I pray for Patty each night.

Date: Friday, February 8, 1974

Topic: Books Kids Should Not Read

Category: Action

Author: Ardenia Dovie Carroll

Location: 727 Rt. 323, Penny Pass, AR

Why, why, WHY, in the world would my parents let me read, "Run, Baby, Run" and "The Cross and the Switchblade"? What were they thinking? I'm 12 for crying out loud. And why, after I read Nicky Cruz's story, did I want to read about Nicky and other gang members from David Wilkerson's point of view? Images of initiations and fights and drugs and sex stuff will never leave my head. I will die with those stories taking up space in my memory bank. When I try to go to sleep, I see ropes and cigarettes and knives and blood and pain and fear.

Date: Saturday, February 9, 1974

Topic: Jacking off

Category: Thing? Action?

Author: Ardenia Dovie Carroll

Location: 727 Rt. 323, Penny Pass, AR

After hearing this phrase many times, I decided to just ask Shep. That's an advantage of having a best friend that's a boy, right? Shep's face has never been that red. I almost said, "I'm sorry" and "forget it" but I didn't. I just stood there. He mumbled something about fluid and penis. Disappointed, I said, "Oh, pee." Then he said, "No, something else." Intrigued, I nodded encouragingly and asked, "How? Why?" to which he simply shook his head and walked away. I called out, "That's just so cool. Like magic." He paused for one split second, didn't turn around, and then continued his walking.

Date: Sunday, February 10, 1974

Topic: Anointing Oil

Category: Thing

Author: Ardenia Dovie Carroll

Location: 727 Rt. 323, Penny Pass, AR

You can anoint with any oil. Olive Oil. Vegetable oil. I've seen Dad pull the dip-stick out from under the car hood and use a bit of that. Anointing someone's head with oil and praying for them comes from scripture. It usually happens when several people are gathered together all praying for the same thing. At church. Someone's home. Outside. It's for when help is needed. Often for healing, but always for help of some kind. I think it's OK to use oil all by yourself, for yourself. A little faith (as little as a grain of mustard seed) along with obedience can go a long ways.

Date: Monday, February 11, 1974

Topic: Lice

Category: Thing

Author: Ardenia Dovie Carroll

Location: 727 Rt. 323, Penny Pass, AR

I didn't want to be rude, but I did not want to sit next to that girl on the bus. Supposedly, she always has lice. We had to sit three to a seat so we were sitting awfully close. I tried not to stare. But I think I saw her hair move. What else could it be? And our coats were touching. So even though it wasn't Tuesday (hair washing day), as soon as I got home, I headed straight for the bathroom. After I ran my bath, I got in. Scrubbed my head. When I got out, I looked, and there, in plain sight, were three gray lice, legs as skinny as my eyelashes, floating in the water. I shuddered.

Date: Tuesday, February 12, 1974

Topic: Quilts

Category: Thing

Author: Ardenia Dovie Carroll

Location: 727 Rt. 323, Penny Pass, AR

Quilts are usually blanket-size. They're made by cutting up old clothes or fabric into small pieces and then sewing them together in a pattern - like Double Wedding Ring, Wild Goose, or Sunbonnet Sue, so there's a theme that runs all the way through. There's often a color theme, too. Mama's making her first: Sunny Lane. We already have lots of quilts given to us over time by church women. I've always liked imagining where the materials came from and making up stories about the people who wore the clothes. When I feel poorly, I go for Touching Stars.

Date: Wednesday, February 13, 1974

Topic: Smooth

Category: Feeling

Author: Ardenia Dovie Carroll

Location: 727 Rt. 323, Penny Pass, AR

After church, I got ready for bed and said good-night. Mama surprised me by coming into my room with the hairbrush and telling me to turn around. I sat on the bed with my fanny on the edge. She stood behind me and brushed my hair until every inch of my scalp had been brushed. Until every hair follicle tingled from attention. When my hair crackled with electricity, we both giggled. Now, my hair is smooth like a worn out puppy. And my mind is smooth like a summer pond. And my heart is smooth like a rose petal. And I believe I shall fall right to sleep.

Date: Thursday, February 14, 1974,

Topic: Zeke Ferguson (Ezekiel Leon Ferguson)

Category: People

Author: Ardenia Dovie Carroll

Location: 727 Rt. 323, Penny Pass, AR

Zeke's hair is feathered and full and brown. Like his eyes. He has a habit of pushing his hair out of his face. But not straight back. More from way back on the left side of his head all the way over to the right side. He has what I think is meant by an easy smile. Of course, he's handsome. But not just on the outside. On the inside, too. He sticks up for people who are bullied. He's nice to the lunch ladies (who give him extra peanut butter cornflake bars). He's born again and comes to our church sometimes. He might like me. I hope he does. He's 14 and tall. I'd like to call him my Valentine.

Date: Friday, February 15, 1974

Topic: Summer in Winter

Category: Thing, Place

Author: Ardenia Dovie Carroll

Location: 727 Rt. 323, Penny Pass, AR

Mom started to make peach turnovers but, at the last minute, did something better. She made enough pie crust for a double. Instead of rolling it out thin, she left it kind of thick and instead of putting it in a pan to bake, she laid it out on a cookie sheet. Then she dotted it with butter, and sprinkled it with cinnamon and sugar. Baked it till it was golden. She whipped heavy cream until the peaks rose and stood firm and high. For dessert, she spooned last summer's peaches over broken-up pie crust and dolloped rich cream on the top. We drooled when she set it down. Heavenly.

Date: Saturday, February 16, 1974

Topic: Lovebirds

Category: People

Author: Ardenia Dovie Carroll

Location: 727 Rt. 323, Penny Pass, AR

A cold rainy day. Spit snow off and on. Mom and Dad let me stay home today when they went into town for Mom's beauty shop appointment and to get groceries. This doesn't happened often. I'm hardly ever alone. They take their parenting responsibilities seriously. I read all day. When they blew in, they were cold, but happy. I think they liked being alone most of the day. Daddy helped put away the groceries before he went to his study and Mama hummed while she cooked dinner. They went to bed early and when I crept by their door, I heard snuggling noises.

Date: Sunday, February 17, 1974

Topic: End Days

Category: Thing

Author: Ardenia Dovie Carroll

Location: 727 Rt. 323, Penny Pass, AR

This is what's referred to in the very last book of the Bible, Revelation. The End. Revelation reveals clues about what life will be like right before The Second Coming of Jesus. But it can't come right out and tell you everything perfectly because although they were prophesying they weren't told how the 1970's would be. So you have to read it, translate, and then fit it with life now. Everyone seems to be looking at what's wrong with the world. Some say things are getting worse. Don't be scared, but these are the End Days. Try to pray without ceasing even if that's tricky.

Date: Monday, February 18, 1974

Topic: Cold

Category: Feeling

Author: Ardenia Dovie Carroll

Location: 727 Rt. 323, Penny Pass, AR

Still cold, still wet. Mama says it's the kind of cold you can't shake. You shiver from your spine out and get tired from the shaking but can't stop. So at the end of the day, you're just worn out. We were all worn out tonight. I did my homework sitting in front of the furnace. My face was hot to the touch. Mom wrapped a blanket around her feet. Daddy placed eight bricks on the furnace. When they were hot, he wrapped them in an old towel and took them out to Dilly's dog house. When he got back in, he didn't take off his coat for a whole hour.

Date: Tuesday, February 19, 1974

Topic: Wondrous Sitings in the Hymnal

Category: Poetry - Accidental

Author: Ardenia Dovie Carroll

Location: 727 Rt. 323, Penny Pass, AR

I will sing the <u>wondrous</u> story of the
Christ who died for me.
Everybody ought to know the <u>wondrous</u>
love of Jesus.
Everywhere behold the <u>wonders</u> of His Grace.
I know not why
God's <u>wondrous</u> Grace to me He hath made known.
Whosoever,
Drink of the fullness
Jesus shall give.
Sing the <u>wondrous</u> love of Jesus.
Heaven's Grace can never fail.

Date: Wednesday, February 20, 1974

Topic: Mama's Windowsill

Category: Place

Author: Ardenia Dovie Carroll

Location: 727 Rt. 323, Penny Pass, AR

In the kitchen, there's a window over the sink. When Mama stands there, she can look outside. Past the dog pen, and the hog pen, and to the woods behind the church's girls outhouse. Sometimes, whatever she's seeing, it's like she's never seen it before. Sometimes she's looking but doesn't seem to be seeing. Anyway, every night after dishes, she uses the wrung-out washrag to clean her windowsill. She lifts her little coral blossomed cactus, her eager donkey tail plant, and the white gardenia candle that she never burns. Each evening she swipes the daily dust off the candle's top.

Date: Thursday, February 21, 1974

Topic: Sucker

Category: Thing

Author: Ardenia Dovie Carroll

Location: 727 Rt. 323, Penny Pass, AR

Zeke is being very nice to me. He's been smiling whenever he sees me. Of course, I smile right back. Today, he walked me down the halls to my classes a couple of times. This afternoon, Shep got off the bus first. I was following him and Zeke was following me. As I was going down the steps, Zeke poked me with something. It was a square cinnamon sucker that I slipped in my pocket for later. When I said thanks he said it wasn't anything. But it is.

Date: Friday, February 22, 1974

Topic: What to do?

Category: Action

Author: Ardenia Dovie Carroll

Location: 727 Rt. 323, Penny Pass, AR

Friday! Yeah! No homework so here are some things
I could do this weekend: Clean out my drawers.
Look through pictures. Read. Bake something new.
Bake something old. Sneak Dilly into my room.
Look through Daddy's bookshelves. Organize the
little kids' Sunday School cabinet. Polish the pews
until they shine. Memorize a passage of scripture.
See if somebody can come over between services
on Sunday to hang out. After eenie meenie miney
moe, pictures win. I bet Mama joins me. I bet she
tells stories. Some I've heard, but maybe new ones,
too.

Date: Saturday, February 23, 1974

Topic: Mama's Fingers and Hands

Category: People

Author: Ardenia Dovie Carroll

Location: 727 Rt. 323, Penny Pass, AR

All of the fingers on each of my hands work as one unit. It's clear they're an extension of my hand, which they obey. But each of Mama's fingers has its own mind. Think Thumbkin, Pointer, Tallman, Ringo, and Pinky. Each finger works as an individual. And, together, as a team. Kneading bread, snapping beans, removing splinters, buttoning, tying, sorting, folding, holding. Strong fingers, subdivided by knuckles, wrapped in vein vines, and covered by mother skin. Fingers that bend, flex, curl, push, pull, spread, and shape. Fine, fine fingers on fine, fine hands. My Mama's Fingers and Hands.

Date: Sunday, February 24, 1974

Topic: Temptation

Category: Thing, Feeling, Place

Author: Ardenia Dovie Carroll

Location: 727 Rt. 323, Penny Pass, AR

It isn't temptation unless it is something you really want. Right this very minute. Satan tempted Jesus when He was hungry and at a real low point to turn stones into bread, to just jump and let the angels catch him, and to worship Satan in exchange for all the kingdoms in the world. Jesus must have known that changing his immediate circumstances in any way would get in the way of the bigger picture. So he rode temptation like a surfer dude rides waves. Waves can take you under but eventually, they spill upon the shore and their power is over.

Date: Monday, February 25, 1974

Topic: Zeke

Category: Person

Author: Ardenia Dovie Carroll

Location: 727 Rt. 323, Penny Pass, AR

Zeke and I might just be good friends but it could be more! When I see him, I feel extra happy. And I want to go out of my way to see him. I like it when he smiles. I like when he talks. I feel lucky that we go to the same school. That he knows I'm alive. That he thinks I am interesting. I think he does. I like that he asks me questions. That he's easy to talk to - even though I still feel shy or embarrassed sometimes. I like how he walks. How he holds his books. I like how, when he laughs, his shoulders laugh, too. How his run is easy, and effortless.

Date: Tuesday, February 26, 1974

Topic: Bread

Category: Thing

Author: Ardenia Dovie Carroll

Location: 727 Rt. 323, Penny Pass, AR

Bread. I love it. A lot. "<u>Man</u> cannot live by bread alone" but perhaps <u>I, as an almost woman, could</u>. As for real bread, there's white, wheat, rye, toast, biscuits, banana, Kings Hawaiian, zucchini, croissants, muffins, rolls, garlic, monkey, cornbread, croutons, buns, and date nut. Pizza and big, soft pretzels might be bread. I had a scone once that was a mix between a biscuit and a cookie. There's bread pudding. Which should be banned. Have one or the other! Then, there's the bread not of this world: Communion bread and the very best of all – The Bread of Life (which is Jesus).

Date: Wednesday, February 27, 1974

Topic: Skipping

Category: Action

Author: Ardenia Dovie Carroll

Location: 727 Rt. 323, Penny Pass, AR

It's ok to skip a day, or even two, of writing cards. When I determined that I was going to keep a card catalog and that I'd write one card a day, I was just stating a goal and a way to achieve it. Skipping a day isn't the end of the world. Sometimes, I might be busy. Or really tired. Or, I might need a little extra time to think. On the other hand, writing more than one card a day is fine, too. Twelve lines just might not cut it. Or I might just <u>want</u> to write more. One card a day is good practice; but it isn't a commandment.

Date: Thursday, February 28, 1974

Topic: Cussing and Fighting

Category: Action

Author: Ardenia Dovie Carroll

Location: 727 Rt. 323, Penny Pass, AR

I heard awful language today. I shouldn't write it but I'm going to. Two guys broke out in a fist fight. Before they were taken by teachers to the principal's office, they'd called each other: Bastard. Asshole. Prick. G------ Asshole. Fucking Lunatic. Pussy. Their arms were swinging 90 to nothing. They were huffing. Punches landed on faces, stomachs, ribs, arms. When the first guy was pulled away, he kicked, and a nose was bloodied. It was upsetting but exciting, too. At dinner I told a watered-down version. Without any cussing, of course. It seemed like I'd not told the story at all.

March
1974

Date: Friday, March 1 (why keep writing the year?)

Topic: Mother Goose and Mother Ruby

Category: People, Thing

Author: Ardenia Dovie Carroll

Location: 727 Rt. 323, Penny Pass, AR

When I was little, Mama would singsong a rhyme for me. It was nice to hear her voice. It was doubly nice because the rhyme had my name in it. It's the only other place I've ever heard my name. "Oh Ardenia, my lil Gardenia, how do your flowers grow? With silver bells, and cockle shells, and pretty maids all in a row." It was years before I knew the original was "Mary, Mary, quite contrary." Sometimes I still ask her, "Where's my Mother Ruby?" because I know she'll start the rhyme. Sometimes I want to be hugged by her voice as well as her arms.

Date: Saturday, March 2

Topic: Juicy

Category: Action, Feeling, Place

Author: Ardenia Dovie Carroll

Location: 727 Rt. 323, Penny Pass, AR

I overheard a lady talking about how juicy something was. You'd have thought it had to do with food, but you'd be wrong. She was talking about life! She spoke of taking a trip, being above the earth in a plane, people she met, beds she slept in, music, dancing. Sunshine. Stars and moon "shine". With both hands circling around to help her find her words, she said, "It was just so. . . so. . . so. . . juicy!" Then both women laughed - one because of her own experience, the other with delight for the storyteller, and bright bursts of light charged the air around them.

Date: Sunday, March 3

Topic: Rock Bottom

Category: Place

Author: Ardenia Dovie Carroll

Location: 727 Rt. 323, Penny Pass, AR

Today we had a guest preacher and Daddy sat in the pew with Mama and me. The preacher told his life story. How he'd been hell-bent (Daddy frowned. It sounded mighty close to cussing.) on drinking, carousing, and gambling with his very life. How one night, in the middle of throwing up and throw up, he hit rock bottom. In deep despair, he called out for mercy. "God, help me," he cried, still throwing up. And God brought him out of the slops of sin, the swamps of shame, the sludge of selfishness. Set him free, put a song in his heart, a spring to his steps. His shimmy gave Daddy another frown.

Date: Monday, March 4

Topic: The Heavy Side

Category: Thing

Author: Ardenia Dovie Carroll

Location: 727 Rt. 323, Penny Pass, AR

It isn't nice to say someone is fat. We say they're
on the heavy side. Leaning toward the heavy side
means plump. A little on the heavy side means
somewhat fat. We have a lady in our church who
is way over on the heavy side. She stays holed
up. Which means she doesn't go out much. Mama
says it's a circle. "She doesn't move around much,
so she's on the heavy side, so moving around is
harder so she just stays put." "Within an arm's
reach of potato chips," Daddy added. "*Collie!*" Mama
exclaimed but she grinned and shook her head. Then
Daddy got up to see if we had any Ruffles.

Date: Tuesday, March 5

Topic: ~~Slow~~ Determination

Category: Person

Author: Ardenia Dovie Carroll

Location: 727 Rt. 323, Penny Pass, AR

After school, there's this kid who lines up for the bus one over from mine. He's slow. And determined. While kids scuffle around him, guys punching one another, girls laughing, shrieking, he kneels on the ground and digs with a metal spoon that I think came from the cafeteria. Each day his hole gets just a little bit deeper. It's deep enough now to sprain an ankle. After it rains, he scoops the muddy water out with his hands. Today, I leaned down and asked him, "Why do you dig?" With a dreamy smile and faraway eyes, he paused and said, "China." I made an A-O-K sign and left him to it.

Date: Wednesday, March 6

Topic: I Saw the Light

Category: Action

Author: Ardenia Dovie Carroll

Location: 727 Rt. 323, Penny Pass, AR

An elder stood up to testify tonight. He's so frail, it took him a while to stand up and get his feet under him good. His shaky hands held the pew in front of him. He wore a plain white ironed dress shirt and striped bib overalls. His pocket watch chain inched into a deep pocket. I can't remember what he said. While he spoke, though, he stood up straighter. He raised one hand in praise. Then, he let go and danced a 3-second shuffle. His soft turkey wattle moved like rippling water. Others smiled and Amen-ed him. I found tears on my cheeks.

Date: Thursday, March 7

Topic: The Waltons

Category: People, Thing

Author: Ardenia Dovie Carroll

Location: 727 Rt. 323, Penny Pass, AR

On Thurs nights, The Waltons show airs on CBS. It's Mama's and my favorite show. Dad likes it: It's "wholesome". He thumbs through magazines while it's on. Mama often folds clothes — because she barely has to glance down. I like to watch laying on the floor. Close to the TV. Mama and Daddy sometimes say they "watch me watch television" and I don't want them to. Tears might sprout from my eyes. The Waltons are a big, loving family with good values. They work through problems, and support each other. John-boy is a writer. Each episode begins and closes with his voice.

Date: Friday, March 8

Topic: Crooning Love's Tune

Category: Action

Author: Ardenia Dovie Carroll

Location: 727 Rt. 323, Penny Pass, AR

Sounding like what Mama calls a righteous brother, Daddy belted out this tonight: "Hey Baby! I love you so. A-hey Baby! Let's go. Let's go sailin' on my boat by the light of the silver-r-y moon. (Dad twists a bit and snaps a few times.) By the li-i-ight of the silvery mo-oo-oon, I-I-I-I want to spoon, to my honey I'll croon love's tune, Woa-oh-oh, honeymoon, keep a-shinin' in June, Your silvery beams will bring love dreams, We'll be cuddlin' so-oo-oo-oo-on by the silvery moooon." He winked at the end and Mama shook her head but she was grinning when she pressed her hand to her heart.

Date: Saturday, March 9

Topic: Breastfeeding

Category: Action

Author: Ardenia Dovie Carroll

Location: 727 Rt. 323, Penny Pass, AR

Not a lot of moms do this. Most use a bottle but in town today, I saw a woman breastfeeding her baby. For a second, when the baby yanked away the blankie, I saw her full, large breast and dark nipple. Mom and Dad saw, too. Mama murmured "privacy" but she smiled. We got in the car, and Daddy said, "That was what God intended all along, Ardenia. It used to be common. No one thought a thing about it. People act like it's a sin to feed a baby. Or uncouth. Maybe someday it will be easy again. I hope you think about that when you have babies." I was more than a bit surprised.

Date: Sunday, March 10

Topic: Eternity

Category: Place

Author: Ardenia Dovie Carroll

Location: 727 Rt. 323, Penny Pass, AR

It's longer than you can imagine. Infinity boggles the human mind. Anything that goes on forever and ever is naturally unconceivable to us. We talk more about spending eternity in hell than in heaven because once you're in heaven, you can relax with relief. In hell, no matter how sorry you are, or how much pain you are in from constantly burning, you're stuck. Imagining spending eternity in hell causes people to reconsider how they spend their finite days here. None of us know when we'll go, so it's better to be safe than sorry.

Date: Monday, March 11

Topic: Breastfeeding, continued

Category: Action

Author: Ardenia Dovie Carroll

Location: 727 Rt. 323, Penny Pass, AR

Mom and Dad surprise me sometimes. Do all parents? After all the talk about keeping our bodies covered, he said what he did about breast-feeding. I guess when your body is uncovered to care for a baby, it is ok. If you're doing it to get someone's attention, to flirt, or even to stay cool, it's not. If someone has sinful or lustful thoughts about breasts that are feeding a baby, I guess the sin would be their fault and not the woman's. I guess taking care of babies is more important than making sure you don't cause someone to sin.

Date: Tuesday, March 12

Topic: My 2nd Period. (Perspective)

Category: Thing

Author: Ardenia Dovie Carroll

Location: 727 Rt. 323, Penny Pass, AR

I started my period at school. At school! Unlucky!
I felt a little something happening down there and
I raised my hand right away. Luckily, I got dismissed right away and got to the bathroom before
it was too much. Luckily, I had change in my shoe
for a pad. Luckily, I was wearing my dark green
pants. So I just sat prim and proper the rest of
the day, keeping my legs pressed together at the
knees. Luckily, they didn't stain. Luckily, I kept my
cool. Luckily, Mama made brownies today. Luckily,
when she heard about my day, she let me have
two.

Date: Wednesday, March 13

Topic: Bored

Category: Feeling

Author: Ardenia Dovie Carrol

Location: 727 Rt. 323, Penny Pass, AR

I'm not bored with God or the Bible. I'm bored with how we always spend Wed nights. But Daddy says, "don't complain if you don't also have a solution." So tonight, I tuned him out and thought about what we could do instead. I came up with: 1) A talent show. 2) Just sing for an hour and a half and go home. 3) Ask one question and let everybody answer it. Like: What was one time God answered your prayer? (Be sure to set a timer. Some folks are sure to hog the time.) 4) Take turns telling testimonies. Feature one person a night. Think about all of the stories!

Date: Thursday, March 14

Topic: Mom on the Phone

Category: Person

Author: Ardenia Dovie Carroll

Location: 727 Rt. 323, Penny Pass, AR

When Mom is on the phone, she pulls the receiver around the hallway corner and momentarily perches on the arm of our tan naugahyde couch. I call that spot her perch. She flips her kitchen towel over her shoulder. She fiddles with its fringe. Scrapes off dried jelly, flicks off flecks of toast. She stands and steps over to the TV cabinet and dusts a bit with her hand or a clean spot of towel. She perches again, checking the skin on the back of each hand. Rises. Holds the receiver between cheek and shoulder, straightens the quilt on the couch. Dad calls this phone-fiddling.

Date: Friday, March 15

Topic: Me on the Phone. And Dad, too.

Category: Person

Author: Ardenia Dovie Carroll

Location: 727 Rt. 323, Penny Pass, AR

When I'm on the phone, I stretch the cord, hold it pretty tight, slip into my room, and close the door. I might toss a pillow on the hardwood floor, lay down, and stretch my legs up the wall, pointing my toes, twisting my ankles. Or, I sit with my back against the door, drawing my knees up until I am a perfect backward N. Tirelessly, I twist a thin section of my hair, tying it into a special knot that instantly springs and unravels when I let go. For Dad, there's no phone-fiddling. He grows roots and horse blinders and stands stark still and looks straight at the phone hanging on the wall.

Date: Saturday, March 16

Topic: Good Housekeeping

Category: Thing, People

Author: Ardenia Dovie Carroll

Location: 727 Rt. 323, Penny Pass, AR

This month features The Kienast Quintuplets and Billie Jean King. The quints are now 4 years old. They were the first U.S. set of quints who survived after being conceived with fertility drugs (which help moms who have trouble having babies). Billie Jean is a tennis star and a women's libber. She says women should be treated like men. Last year she beat Bobby Riggs, who disagreed with her. He'd said that women's tennis was so low that at the age 55 he could beat the best of them. He couldn't. She said she HAD to win. For women everywhere.

Date: Sunday, March 17

Topic: Praise

Category: Thing

Author: Ardenia Dovie Carroll

Location: 727 Rt. 323, Penny Pass, AR

Tonight at the end of the service, we praised God for more than 30 minutes. I know, I shouldn't concern myself about the time. Daddy walked back and forth across the stage, waving his arms and weeping. "We just love ya, Lord." "You're just so good to us." Caught up in the Spirit, it was like he was in a trance. After a bit, people started leaving. They might have been watching the clock, too. Mama, like always, sat still, eyes closed, only her lips moving. I would have sworn (if I could), with one big sigh, she murmured, "Lord, I just wanna go home."

Date: Monday, March 18

Topic: Christ Ambassadors

Category: People

Author: Ardenia Dovie Carroll

Location: 727 Rt. 323, Penny Pass, AR

Basically, Christ Ambassadors are teenagers who want to help win souls for Christ. The song explains: "We are Christ Ambassadors, and our colors (blue and gold) we must unfurl. We must wear a spotless robe, clean and righteous before the world. We must show we're cleansed from sin, and that Jesus dwells within. Proving duly that we're truly Christ Am-bas-sa-dors." Christ for All; All for Christ. At CA Rallies, CA's meet CA's from other churches and have a lot of fun. Everyone arrives on buses. On the way back home, the teens who sit in the very back of the bus kiss.

Date: Tuesday, March 19

Topic: Make-Up

Category: Thing

Author: Ardenia Dovie Carroll

Location: 727 Rt. 323, Penny Pass, AR

Daddy says "painted" ladies are up to no good. Example: Jezebel. She was a princess; a painted lady; she persuaded her husband to worship a false god; she lied, stole, and arranged murder. Therefore, she died a terrible death. A horse trampled her head. Then wild dogs ate her flesh. Beautiful women have a lot of power, especially when they are full of the devil. Men become mere puppets, doing only whatever the lady proposes. Me? I'd just like to wear mascara even though it comes from bat poop. And a little pink lipstick because pink looks good on me.

Date: Wednesday, March 20

Topic: Bible Drills

Category: Thing

Author: Ardenia Dovie Carroll

Location: 727 Rt. 323, Penny Pass, AR

Before the drill, the leader (who can be a kid) comes up with a whole list of Bible verses. Usually they are all connected in some way. The leader calls out a scripture and everyone scrambles to be the first one to find it. When you find it, don't be shy! Stand up immediately and begin to read. Unless someone else is already reading. When it's been read, the next one will be called out. Sometimes the leader explains how the scriptures work together but I like it better when they don't. That's part of the challenge. I like to figure it out on my own.

Date: Thursday. March 21

Topic:

Category:

Author: Ardenia Dovie Carroll

Location:

Date: Friday, March 22

Topic: The Blue Dream

Category: Thing

Author: Ardenia Dovie Carroll

Location: 727 Rt. 323, Penny Pass, AR

I dreamt I was at the bottom of a column. Like a very tall silo. I was lying flat on my back, looking up at the sky through the open circle above me. Beneath me, around me, above me (except for that small circle overhead) - all was dark. The top of the silo was so far above me that my fist could block out the entire circle and view of the sky. It was so far above me that the sky seemed to be just a flat blue disc placed on top. Like a lid. As long as I kept looking at that blue, I felt ok. So, I fixed my eyes on blue and waited.

Date: Saturday, March 23

Topic: Mom's Hair Washing

Category: Action

Author: Ardenia Dovie Carroll

Location: 727 Rt. 323, Penny Pass, AR

Mom lets down her hair every Saturday morning.
She removes a bajillion bobby pins and hair pins,
brushes from the ends first and then moves up a
few inches at a time until her hair is clear of the
rats that were backcombed in the Saturday
before. She leans over the kitchen sink, washes
twice, conditions once, rinses until her dark hair
squeaks, and twists the towel around her head.
She wears the towel around her shoulders while
her hair dries. At 1:30, she ties a scarf around her
head and Dad takes her to her standing beauty
shop appointment.

Date: Sunday, March 24

Topic: Grace and Responsibility

Category: Action

Author: Ardenia Dovie Carroll

Location: 727 Rt. 323, Penny Pass, AR

Grace is unwarranted favor. Deserving one thing and getting something much better. I've heard Dad preach on grace many times. But what would grace be in practical terms? Grace would be eating at the cafeteria when you have no money to pay. Or being given an A when you earned a D. But, is the <u>reason</u> any consideration at all? Is penniless-ness more "deserving" of grace than blowing your lunch money on new clothes? Is studying hard more deserving than shirking? If so, wouldn't grace be even more grace in the last examples?

Date: Monday, March 25

Topic: Cagey

Category: Person

Author: Ardenia Dovie Carroll

Location: 727 Rt. 323, Penny Pass, AR

There's another kid who does his own thing after school. Unlike the boy who's digging his way to China, this guy stands apart from everyone. One eye slightly closed. Squinting just a tad. If you catch his eye, he juts out his chin. Like "What are YOU looking at?" I don't know what his problem is but I do know that Jesus loves him. Today, when he jutted, I smiled. He looked away. When he looked back I was still smiling, even bigger. He reminds me of a dog that's been kicked around. You have to go real slow because they don't know who to trust.

Date: Tuesday, March 26

Topic: Change

Category: Action

Author: Ardenia Dovie Carroll

Location: 727 Rt. 323, Penny Pass, AR

It only happens with dress pants. Not with Daddy's jeans. But when Daddy goes to any church service, you will, at some point, find him standing around with other men. All of them will have at least one hand in a pocket, sieving change through their fingers. If you are quiet and close your eyes for a moment and focus, you can imagine numerous small, but weighty, metal, wind chimes blown about by gusts of large calloused hands.

Date: Wednesday, March 27

Topic: Counting

Category: Action

Author: Ardenia Dovie Carroll

Location: 727 Rt. 323, Penny Pass, AR

Tonight I counted. 34 purses and 17 umbrellas were carried. 13 hats worn. 63 people at church. 4 songs sung. 7 scriptural references. Mom smoothed her hair 11 times during the service. Daddy walked back and forth across the stage 17 times. Shep poked me 6 times. The toddler in front of us rammed his finger up his nose 9 times (Shep poked me 5 of these.) and pulled out a bloody finger just once. Sister Ella nodded off twice. Brother Ben snored once, right before Sister Clara elbowed him. Lightning flashed 4 times. The power flickered off twice.

Date: Thursday, March 28

Topic: Ouija Board

Category: Thing

Author: Ardenia Dovie Carroll

Location: 727 Rt. 323, Penny Pass, AR

Sales are up. You can sell your soul for only 3 bucks. Of course, I haven't played with one, nor have I seen one, but I've heard (from kids who go to our church and have heard Daddy preach!) that it's a regular game board with letters. The players put their hands on these moving parts and, without any effort, words are spelled out. Spirits, ghosts, or more likely old Lucifer himself takes over and tells you something he wants you to think. Beware! All it takes is one unprotected opening for devil possession. And this, for $3. It just ought to be outlawed.

Date: Friday, March 29

Topic: Just a Kid

Category: Action

Author: Ardenia Dovie Carroll

Location: 727 Rt. 323, Penny Pass, AR

Somebody started singing "99 Bottles of Beer on the Wall" on the bus this afternoon. Then most everyone was singing away. Heads swinging back and forth in time. It was everything I could do to not sing. If only it had been milk. When I glared at Shep (he was singing, too) he said, "It's a <u>song</u>. I ain't <u>drinking</u> the beer," and continued to sing. It's at times like this I feel odd and old and alone. It's hard to be an example. To do the right thing, <u>all</u> the time. Sometimes I just want to be a regular kid singing like there's no tomorrow, like there's no heaven, and certainly like there's no hell.

Date: Saturday, March 30

Topic: Public Peeing

Category: Action

Author: Ardenia Dovie Carroll

Location: 727 Rt. 323, Penny Pass, AR

Each Saturday, I look for the breastfeeding mother so I can show her I support her. I'm not sure how I'd do this. But I haven't seen her. Today, though, I saw something else. I saw a man stumble to the edge of the parking lot, turn most of the way around, unzip his britches, and start peeing. My feet were instantly glued to the asphalt. Then Dad barked my name. I said, "I bet that used to be commonplace, too." I was doing everything I could to watch out of the corners of my eyes but Dad barked again. Mama and I walked straight to our car and Daddy went over to help.

Date: Sunday, March 31

Topic: Quarterly Card Catalog Update

Category: Thing, Action

Author: Ardenia Dovie Carroll

Location: 727 Rt. 323, Penny Pass, AR

Three months of card keeping finds me just as devoted as I was on January 1st. There is no shortage of things to write about. If I had to fill a whole 8½ x 11 page, I'm pretty sure I'd get lazy. Either by meandering around la-de-dah on the page just to fill it up or I'd just stop before completing. These cards keep me sharp. And on my toes. Attention! They demand I choose something <u>before</u> I start writing, demand I not ramble on and on while I write. And then, all of a sudden, the bottom of the card is here, demanding I wrap it up, and quick.

April
1974

Date: Monday, April 1

Topic: My 13th Birthday

Category: People

Author: Ardenia Dovie Carroll

Location: 727 Rt. 323, Penny Pass, AR

I'm an April Fool's day baby, so I've heard those jokes since I started school. Daddy and Mama say I'm their April <u>Angel</u> baby. We always choose our own birthday dinners. This year, I chose spaghetti and meatballs and garlic bread. Chocolate cake with chocolate icing. Vanilla ice cream. After I made a wish (I can't speak <u>or</u> write it) and blew out the candles, Daddy grabbed me like he was going to give me my birthday spanking with one to grow on but Mama touched his arm and said, "Maybe not, Collie." I was disappointed and I could tell Daddy was, too. She said, "What about a birthday <u>hug</u>?"

Date: Tuesday, April 2

Topic: Nightgown

Category: Thing

Author: Ardenia Dovie Carroll

Location: 727 Rt. 323, Penny Pass, AR

Nylon nightgowns build up electricity. When you flip over in bed, you can hear sparks. Lift the blanket quickly, and you can see them flash. I found this nightgown in the Sears catalog. When Mama asked what I wanted for my birthday, I told her the blue one (even though I look good in pink). It was a surprise to get the matching robe, too. They are long (all the way to my ankle) and soft and swingy. When I wear them, I feel like I'm playing dress up and being grown up, all at the same time. The pale blue matches the teeny five-petaled flowers that spring up everywhere in summer.

Date: Wednesday, April 3

Topic: Mascara

Category: Thing

Author: Ardenia Dovie Carroll

Location: 727 Rt. 323, Penny Pass, AR

It's made from bat poop. Let's just say that first. But, it makes your eyelashes look fuller and longer. So it might be worth it. I do not know if it smells in any way like poop of any kind. Haven't been close enough to any to sniff. Eyelashes that are mascaraed look heavy and you notice them more. You can buy it in brown or black. I think I'd get black. Some days my bottom lashes seem longer than my top lashes. I could just mascara the top lashes to balance out my eyes. But I might put two coats on top and only one on the bottom. I sure do wish Daddy would say, "yes."

Date: Thursday, April 4

Topic: Cookies

Category: Action

Author: Ardenia Dovie Carroll

Location: 727 Rt. 323, Penny Pass, AR

I tell everyone I bake cookies for our principal because his wife has left him and his little boy for another man and I feel sorry for him. And I do. But he's also very handsome. I store the cookies, wrapped in foil, in my locker until after school. Then I run them over to his house before my bus takes off. He's never home, of course. He's still in his office but he leaves his front door unlocked because he can see it from his desk chair. I dash in, place the cookies on his counter, and take a quick look. He does his own dishes. His morning glory suncatcher greets me with cobalt blue.

Date: Friday, April 5

Topic: My Whole Life Long Songs

Category: Thing

Author: Ardenia Dovie Carroll

Location: 727 Rt. 323, Penny Pass, AR

"Tu-ra-lu-ra-lu-ra, tu-ra-lu-ra-li, tu-ra-lu-ra-lu-ra. Hush now, don't you cry. Tu-ra-lu-ra-lu-ra, tu-ra-lu-ra-li, tu-ra-lu-ra-lu-ra, just an Irish lullaby." I've heard this my whole life. That, and "The bear went over the mountain" and "He's got the whole world in his hands" and "Mairzy doats" and "Buffalo gals" and "Make new friends, but keep the old, one is silver and the other's gold" and "My little Kat-ll-ate-e-eey" and "You are my sunshine" and "Where have you been, Billy boy, Billy boy?" and "I wonder what became of Sally" and "The old grey mare, she ain't what she used to be" and so many more.

Date: Saturday, April 6

Topic: Easter Dress

Category: Thing

Author: Ardenia Dovie Carroll

Location: 727 Rt. 323, Penny Pass, AR

Well, this is a first. Mama hasn't sewn our Easter dresses. "Let's splurge!" she said. I know it's because she hasn't had the time to sew - between the funerals, casseroles, tears and hugs and hours with sad people. Daddy took us shopping today. With each dress, he gave a thumbs up or down. Usually regarding dress lengths or necklines. We found Mama a yellow dress, with a tiny belt. She looked like a rose. I wasn't so lucky. I ended up with brown. Brown! For Easter! Like Dad's pants. Or poop. But I said thank you and I'll wear it like it's what I've always wanted.

Date: Sunday, April 7

Topic: Slain Under the Spirit

Category: Thing, Action

Author: Ardenia Dovie Carroll

Location: 727 Rt. 323, Penny Pass, AR

If you don't know anything about it, you might be surprised when it happens. Usually, someone comes to the front for prayer. Then the Holy Spirit comes through the preacher and slays the other person, who then slumps to the ground, usually to their back or to one side. Sometimes, we are prepared for this. A deacon stands behind the person in order to catch them and lay them down gently. When women are being prayed for, other women stand ready with sweaters or baby blankies to make sure their slain sisters are covered up at least down to their knees.

Date: Monday, April 8

Topic: Spring Break

Category: Action

Author: Ardenia Dovie Carroll

Location: 727 Rt. 323, Penny Pass, AR

It's great to be out of school but the rain has us holed up. Held up. Dad said, "When life gives you lemons, make lemonade." Mom said, "Make the best of it," as she followed Daddy into their bedroom to take a nap. I watched the rain for a while. The sky was glummy gray, not that beautiful blue gray I like. The gray that's the color of Full. Full of Activity and Heavy with Possibility. Today's gray was grungy. Boring. Annoying. Then Shep asked if I wanted to "play" in the rain. We stomped, splashed, slid, squeaked, and snorted gray today.

Date: Tuesday, April 9

Topic: Spring Rain

Category: Action

Author: Ardenia Dovie Carroll

Location: 727 Rt. 323, Penny Pass, AR

It's still raining. Shep and I decided to see how many board games we could play. We started at his house. I'd never played Battleship and I hope I never do again. We postponed Monopoly because it takes so long. We'll save that in case it's still raining in a few days. Yahtzee, Operation, Dominoes. Twister (which was a little weird). Then we came over here. We played Pick Up Sticks, Aggravation, Chinese Checkers, Barrel of Monkeys, and Candyland just to be silly. We made grilled cheese sandwiches with so much cheese it oozed out the sides. We had a good day.

Date: Wednesday, April 10

Topic: Spring Break, Spring Rain

Category: Action

Author: Ardenia Dovie Carroll

Location: 727 Rt. 323, Penny Pass, AR

The Game Marathon continued because the darn rain continued. Connect 4. Racko. When we played Perfection, he was hi-lar-i-ous. Shep was trying so hard. The more we played, the sillier we got. Over at the church, we banged around on the piano and dug out the playdough in the little kiddies room. At his house, we popped a mountain of popcorn. After we were stuffed, we had a popcorn fight. After that, we had to pick up "every last piece." We are both hoping tomorrow is sunny. Tonight the back of the church was lined with opened wet umbrellas.

Date: Thursday, April 11

Topic: Picnic-ing

Category: Action

Author: Ardenia Dovie Carroll

Location: 727 Rt. 323, Penny Pass, AR

Chirping birds and growing light woke me. Outside the ground was soggy but the sky was clear. And blue. At 9 am Mom let me call Shep. We dried our bikes, grabbed our fishing poles, and met at the end of the parking lot. He put his tackle box in my basket. Zeke came out as we rode by. We hollered at him to meet us at the pond. He brought his pole but also visqueen (to sit on), 6 bottles of soda pop, and 2 full bags of Lays. We caught nothing. Except sunshine. Freedom. Laughter by the lung full. We waited for fish, for the ground to dry, and for the next punchline.

Date: Friday, April 12

Topic: Love

Category: Action, Feeling

Author: Ardenia Dovie Carroll

Location: 727 Rt. 323, Penny Pass, AR

The three of us shot HORSE at Zeke's basketball goal. They are so much better than me, it isn't even funny. But it was. After supper, we tossed horseshoes in the church side yard until my arm burned. Dad joined us. Then Mama brought a few folding chairs. Shep's mom and dad walked over swinging his little brother between them. Even Zeke's dad who doesn't ever come to our church walked over. He smelled like cigarettes and some-thing else but Daddy only smiled real big, pumped his hand, and handed over the shoes. I loved Daddy a lot right then.

Date: Saturday, April 13

Topic: Resurrection, from John 20, King James

Category: Poetry - Accidental

Author: Ardenia Dovie Carroll

Location: 727 Rt. 323, Penny Pass, AR

"Why weepest thou?"
"I know not where they've laid Him."
"I will not believe."
The doors were shut.
Disciples were assembled.
Then Jesus came and saith,
"Receive me" and
"Peace be unto you."

Date: Easter Sunday, April 14

Topic: UP From the Grave He Arose!

Category: Action

Author: Ardenia Dovie Carroll

Location: 727 Rt. 323, Penny Pass, AR

Because death doesn't have the last, final say. Because God's plan sees through pain, and sorrow, and despair, and darkness. Even the kind of darkness that covers the whole world. Your whole world. Mine. Because there's always more to the story than what we see at the moment. Because Jesus's love is triumphant and victorious. Because God's promises come true. Because light can shine when you least expect it. Because there is no stopping God and good. Because people can't limit God. Because God so loved the world.

Date: Monday, April 15

Topic: My 3rd Period

Category: Thing

Author: Ardenia Dovie Carroll

Location: 727 Rt. 323, Penny Pass, AR

I'm getting the hang of it. Thinking ahead, thinking everything through. Not heading out the door unprepared. But, when we have to buy pads, now it's even more embarrassing to go through the checkout. It's awful when the sackers, who are always teenage guys, pick up the gigantic purple box to put in the paper sack. Everyone pretends that it has nothing to do with girls private parts. Sat, as Mama placed the box on the conveyor belt, Dad asked the sacker what kind of car he drove. Car talk never sounded so good to me; it lasted until the last sack was in the cart. Go, Dad!

Date: Tuesday, April 16

Topic: Haulassin (Haul Ass-ing)

Category: Action

Author: Ardenia Dovie Carroll

Location: 727 Rt. 323, Penny Pass, AR

On the bus I heard a guy say he'd been haul assin'. Before dinner, Dad was perusing the paper. I asked "Hey, what's haulassin?" like it's one word. I wondered: could I get him to say 'ass'? His head whipped around and I thought I'd gone too far. "What'd you say?" I felt pretty bold so I said, "I'm asking you what haulassin means." "Use it in a sentence, Ardenia." Still with a straight face, Me: "He. Was. Haulassin." Dad: "Oh. Well. You know, ass is another word for donkey. And ass is in the Bible. The -ing's on the wrong word there, pal. 'He was haul-ing ass' as in going fast." I had to bite my lip. 'Ass' X 3!

Date: Wednesday, April 17

Topic: My 3rd Period, cont.

Category: Thing

Author: Ardenia Dovie Carroll

Location: 727 Rt. 323, Penny Pass, AR

It's strange. Mama says in time my body will even out and my periods will be regular. As in the amount of time in between them and how long they last and how heavy I flow. This one came and went without much of anything. I didn't feel terrible. And I think it's nearly over already. If my regular turned out to be like this, it'd be a snap. Today, I made blonde brownies. That's chocolate chip cookie dough dumped into a cake pan and baked for 30 minutes at about 325°. Ooey, gooey, chewy, and chocolate. I had three before serving it as dessert.

Date: Thursday, April 18

Topic: Jesus Christ Superstar

Category: Thing

Author: Ardenia Dovie Carroll

Location: 727 Rt. 323, Penny Pass, AR

Daddy says the movie is a mockery: Jesus, our Lord and Savior, as "J.C." and with all that rock and roll "gyrating". I've only seen the commercials. The fringe on the clothes is cool but I don't say so. The songs play on the radio. One reminds me of a cheer. My version just stays in my head, of course, but it plays over and over: "Jesus Christ, Superstar, you're number one and you know you are." (It's true!) Helen Reddy sings the Mary Magdalene song where she's all confused about loving him, wanting him, and being scared of him, too. She wonders what it's all about. Poor girl.

Date: Friday, April 19

Topic: The Storm Cellar

Category: Place

Author: Ardenia Dovie Carroll

Location: 727 Rt. 323, Penny Pass, AR

Playing on the little hilltop as a kid was fun. As a teenager, sitting on top is nice. Going <u>into</u> them is scary at any age. I've never HAD to go in. I've gone in as far as I wanted, which has been to place both feet on the cellar floor, and I raced right back out. With each step down and in, the air got colder around my ankles. I saw spider webs. Water puddles. The inside smelled old, quiet, wet, cool. I can't imagine closing the door and staying! During a tornado, I think a person would have to choose between two scary things and pick the least scary at that second.

Date: Saturday, April 20

Topic: Collie Cade, Jr.

Category: People

Author: Ardenia Dovie Carroll

Location: 727 Rt. 323, Penny Pass, AR

Until today, I didn't even know there was a Collie Cade, Jr.! Mama miscarried when she was pregnant. Deep down, she knew it was a little boy who'd have been named after Daddy. Had "Cade or Junior" lived, he'd be 3 years older than me. I wonder what he would have been like. I asked Mama, "How sad was it for your little bitty baby to die?" Her eyes closed for a whole second. When she looked at me, her face said "very, very sad" but she sighed, and said "must have been God's will" like she had to say it. Then, "I'm so glad I have you, Ardenia." She opened her arms and I hugged her good and hard.

Date: Sunday, April 21

Topic: Perfume

Category: Thing

Author: Ardenia Dovie Carroll

Location: 727 Rt. 323, Penny Pass, AR

Ambush, Charlie, Love's Baby Soft, Tabu, Wind Song. Avon has: Bird of Paradise, Charisma, Cotillion, Hawaiian White Ginger, Occur!, Surreal, Topaz, Sweet Honesty, Rapture (Of course that has me wondering). A woman at church sells Avon. She brings her catalogs and passes them out. She leaves them scattered among the pews. After church, when I pick up candy wrappers, gum foils, notes of all kinds, and the hymnals to place back in their holders, I find them. Dad says with a wink: "By and large, she's hoping to boost her monthly sales. She's got her eye on a pink Cadillac."

Date: Monday, April 22

Topic:

Category:

Author: Ardenia Dovie Carroll

Location:

Date: Tuesday, April 23

Topic: Beauty Review

Category: Thing

Author: Ardenia Dovie Carroll

Location: 727 Rt. 323, Penny Pass, AR

The Beauty Review is an annual event at Skiddy High School. Every girl from 7th grade through 12th can participate. So, I will. Mama has made my dress out of pink dotted Swiss. The tips of my fingers love those little bumpy white dots and she tells me pink is one of my colors. It's a maxi dress, of course. It has puffy sleeves and a scooped neck. Right before I go on stage, I'll smooth my hair and, since I can't wear make-up, I'll pinch my cheeks and scrape my lips with my teeth a few times. For some color. I bet (if I could bet) I'll be nervous.

Date: Wednesday, April 24

Topic: Foot Washing

Category: Thing, Action

Author: Ardenia Dovie Carroll

Location: 727 Rt. 323, Penny Pass, AR

Jesus washed his disciples' feet and He's our example. So Dad called for a good old-fashioned foot washing. The men gathered on one side, up at the front. They dragged the altar over to face their front pew. The women met on the other side, and set folding chairs in a semi-circle to face their pew. Roasting pans, pitchers, and hand towels were divvied up. (Kids watch.) Dad read John 13:1-17. Then they began. Everyone was reverent and humble. No one snickered or said "Eww." Some looked more comfortable than others. I sat where I could see both sides. It all looked like love to me.

Date: Thursday, April 25

Topic: From Matthew 5, King James Version

Category: Poetry - Accidental

Author: Ardenia Dovie Carroll

Location: 727 Rt. 323, Penny Pass, AR

Ye have heard
ye are the light.
Blessed are ye.
Whosoever
is poor in spirit
pure in heart
shall see God.
Blessed are they that mourn.
Be comforted.
God's throne is
Love.
Leave there thy gift.

Date: Friday, April 26

Topic: The Beauty Review

Category: Thing

Author: Ardenia Dovie Carroll

Location: 727 Rt. 323, Penny Pass, AR

I got dressed, Mama put one of her necklaces on me and we left. Numbers were given out first come, first serve. I arrived after 3 other girls, so I was #4. The tags were white heart-shaped paper, glitter lined in gold. We pinned them on our dresses where our right hands touched our right legs. I was as nervous as I thought I'd be. I bit my lips for real. When I strode out from behind the curtain I walked too fast, but I couldn't slow down. That would be obvious. So I just barreled on through. At the three stopping points I barely slowed. I forgot to even smile. I did not place.

Date: Saturday, April 27

Topic: By and Large

Category: Thing (phrase)

Author: Ardenia Dovie Carroll

Location: 727 Rt. 323, Penny Pass, AR

Dad says this about a million times a day. Today, Mom asked him how the potatoes under the house were lasting. He answered, "By and large, they're just about gone." At the dinner table, he talked about Patricia Hearst. "By and large, she's joined 'em." Weather? "By and large, sunny." It's never basically, or mainly, or generally. Oil prices? "By and large, they keep going up." And Nixon: "By and large, he's a crook. They all are." Sonny and Cher? "By and large, they can't sing a lick and are wasting TV time." (I nearly screamed.) Interestingly, he never says it while he's preaching.

Date: Sunday, April 28

Topic: Awe

Category: Feeling

Author: Ardenia Dovie Carroll

Location: 727 Rt. 323, Penny Pass, AR

One might guess that awe and awful are related. That awful means to be full of awe. (Like beautiful). But one would be wrong. Awe is when your mouth drops open, you forget to breathe, and then you breathe really deep. (I guess that can happen with something awful, too.) When it happens because of awe, though, it's because something is really wonderful or beautiful. All of sudden, your body, brain, and heart don't feel quite big enough to contain what you are experiencing. But you want to, so you breathe it in as much as you can. I was awed at tonight's sunset.

Date: Monday, April 29

Topic: ~~Problems~~ Solutions

Category: Place

Author: Ardenia Dovie Carroll

Location: 727 Rt. 323, Penny Pass, AR

Most problems have a solution. Maybe more than one. Or maybe more than one way to _get_ to the solution. At school, we're told to apply ourselves. If we learn what's before us now, we'll be ready for what comes next. At school, we're told to not jump ahead. At church, we state that no problem is too big for God. I try to trust that. To really believe that. Sometimes, though, some situations just look impossible. Too much sadness. Too much wrong. Too far gone. Just too bad. Sometimes, I think we might have to BE the solution. Not wait on God.

Date: Tuesday, April 30

Topic:

Category:

Author: Ardenia Dovie Carroll

Location:

May
1974

Date: Wednesday, May 1

Topic: Seats

Category: Places

Author: Ardenia Dovie Carroll

Location: 727 Rt. 323, Penny Pass, AR

At church tonight, I sat in a completely different place. You'd have thought I had my clothes on backwards. People looked around like I'd made a mistake and they were waiting for me to make it right. But I didn't. I stuck it out. You have to be careful where you sit because people have their favorite spots and they sit there year after year. Heaven help the visitors who plop down in the wrong place. Mama, Daddy, and I silently pray as visitors tentatively choose a seat because it's terrible to be talking about God's love while people are glaring.

Date: Thursday, May 2

Topic: Colors

Category: Place

Author: Ardenia Dovie Carroll

Location: 727 Rt. 323, Penny Pass, AR

Today, it felt so GOOD to be outside. After school, I stretched out on the front porch in the one patch of sunlight. The sky was blue. Bright. There were no clouds. I closed my eyes. And left them closed. The sun warmed my face. I felt small but held. The longer I laid there the more it felt like I was being rocked back and forth in a big old boat. The longer I laid there, the more color I saw in the back of my eyelids. Orange, red, yellow, yes, but also bursts of eggplant purple and Mountain Dew bottle green. For a second at a time, each vivid color felt pure.

Date: Friday, May 3

Topic: Family Favorites

Category: Thing

Author: Ardenia Dovie Carroll

Location: 727 Rt. 323, Penny Pass, AR

At Shep's, they only ever buy vanilla ice cream. They say it's their favorite because it goes with everything. To make it chocolaty, though, Shep has a plan. He brings out the Nestle' Quick tin. We sprinkle until there's a solid coating on the top of our ice cream. We can eat it just like that, with a crunchy top, or we can stir it until it turns into chocolate ice cream. Like that, it tastes almost like store-bought. One of our family's favorite desserts is a treat Daddy used to have as a kid. Chopped bananas in a bowl, sprinkled with brown sugar, and doused with good cold milk. Mmm.

Date: Saturday, May 4

Topic: Food Prices

Category: Thing

Author: Ardenia Dovie Carroll

Location: 727 Rt. 323, Penny Pass, AR

Fuel price isn't the only one that's gone up. Food prices have, too. Scarcity is a sign of the end times. And greed. Looking out for number one instead of being generous at heart. Walter Cronkite (I always want to say Crankout as in cranking out the news) said that food prices are 25% higher than two years ago. So, here's a math word problem: What were the prices in 1972 if the prices of bread, milk, and tomato soup are now 26¢, $1.39, and 10¢? Answers: (If stores rounded down), Bread-19¢. Milk-$1.04. Soup-7¢ Bonus - for extra points: Oreos-41¢ (They're 55¢ now.)

Date: Sunday, May 5

Topic: Greed

Category: Action

Author: Ardenia Dovie Carroll

Location: 727 Rt. 323, Penny Pass, AR

Greed is about me, me, me. What I need, what I want, what I think. More for me. In Matthew 25: 35-46 Jesus teaches that when we do not feed, clothe, or take care of those who need it, we are, in essence, not tending to Him. By denying others, we deny Jesus. I'm not at all sure how to give everything to God and others, trust Him to care for us, while still being responsible. Dad said this morning, "When your response to someone in need is tightening the hold on your wallet, your tenderness, or your love, you're being greedy." I hope I can remember.

Date: Monday, May 6

Topic: M's - 7 x 12

Category: Thing

Author: Ardenia Dovie Carroll

Location: 727 Rt. 323, Penny Pass, AR

Monday, Mom, milk, moo, menu, melon, mustache.
May, March, mix, machine, mascara, model, muster.
Messy, macaroni, mad, malice, Memphis, middle, mud.
Market, mid, moderate, moss, most, mutual, mangle.
Marmalade, morsel, melt, mutter, mare, metal, mask.
Mascot, muscle, member, melody, money, mist, man.
Maine, Massachusetts, map, mug, mow, musty, ma.
Michigan, Minnesota, Missouri, me, my, mum, myth.
Mississippi, Montana, Maryland, mar, mini, midi, maxi.
Moon, mouth, mighty, mission, million, millipede, mend.
Myriad, myrrh, mind, maneuver, monkey, mice, maze.
Marble, march, mandolin, margarine, mite, mend, mine.

Date: Tuesday, May 7

Topic: Familiarity

Category: Thing

Author: Ardenia Dovie Carroll

Location: 727 Rt. 323, Penny Pass, AR

Mama has a jar of buttons. She keeps the old cloudy thing on her side of the dresser. We all add to it. It's bigger than a quart, but smaller than a gallon. When I was little and bored, Mama would tell me, "Let's go get the jar of buttons." We'd dump them all out and I'd sort by color. When I was really little, it was just by general colors. As I got older, I'd divide by more subtle shades. Navy blue, bright blue, medium blue, light blue, turquoise, blue green, etc. I've looked at them and handled them so often that I know just what I'm looking for when we need one. I riffled through them today.

Date: Wednesday, May 8

Topic: MOTHER - a song from Daddy

Category: People

Author: Ardenia Dovie Carroll

Location: 727 Rt. 323, Penny Pass, AR

"M is for the Million things she gave me.
O is that she's only growing Old.
T is for the Tears she shed to save me.
H is for her Heart of purest gold.
E is for her Eyes with love light shining.
R is Right and Right she'll always be.
Put them all together, they spell MOTHER—
A word that means so much to me."

Daddy taught me this when I was a little girl. It's an old, old song that still means a lot to the person who sings it and the person who hears it.

Date: Thursday, May 9

Topic: My 4th Period

Category: Thing

Author: Ardenia Dovie Carroll

Location: 727 Rt. 323, Penny Pass, AR

Yesterday, my pants felt tight. Like there was rope cinched around my waist. I didn't feel like eating dinner last night, but Daddy said growing girls need to eat. He let me go easy though. I woke up early this morning to go pottie, and when I sat down, I felt it flow out. It's still a surprise. To see blood and try to think: "Normal." "Natural." School went ok. When I stand up, I check the seat to see if I've had an accident. I'm not sure what I'd do if I did. What an embarrassment. I'm going to have to pay more attention to what other girls do.

Date: Friday, May 10

Topic: My 4th Period

Category: Thing

Author: Ardenia Dovie Carroll

Location: 727 Rt. 323, Penny Pass, AR

The excitement has worn off and this is only #4.
I slog along, snail-like, imagining the course of my
day made obvious by a long smelly red smudge.
Dribble, drip, drag. I want clean pads all the time,
especially when the blood turns brown, but I only
grab a new one when the pad is full or six hours
old. This time, I have chills. In May! With sweat. Today was the end-of-the-year picnic. With my favorite: baseball. But I didn't play. I didn't even want
to. I wanted to curl up in my shell and moan. I
sat (carefully) on the ground. Sipping 7-up. I had
no idea woman parts could be so burdensome.

Date: Saturday, May 11

Topic: Tiger Beat

Category: Thing

Author: Ardenia Dovie Carroll

Location: 727 Rt. 323, Penny Pass, AR

Tiger Beat is a teen magazine. Donny Osmond and Tony DeFranco are on every cover. Donny, I understand. But not Tony, who's 15 but looks 11. (Donny is 17 and looks 17.) The monthly issues are full of photos and articles about singers and actresses and actors, who are also called "teen idols." This term is unfortunate because having false idols is a sin. I don't worship the featured stars. I just like to learn about them while Mom and Dad get groceries. I watch as they round the aisles and read as fast as I can until their cart hits the checkout area.

Date: Sunday, May 12

Topic: Mother's Day

Category: Thing, People

Author: Ardenia Dovie Carroll

Location: 727 Rt. 323, Penny Pass, AR

On Mother's Day, we give carnations. A woman gets a white one if her own mom has died; a red one if her own mom is alive. I'm not sure why it's the state of the woman's mom that determines the color and not the state of her children. Thursday night, Dad was called to the hospital for a mom whose son had just died. I went with him but I just sat. Daddy patted her shoulder. She cried, "No, no" and "But next weekend is Mother's Day. It was my weekend. He wanted spaghetti." She didn't come to church today but flowers of every color would have been in order.

Date: Monday, May 13

Topic: Happy as a ~~Clown~~ Clam

Category: Feeling

Author: Ardenia Dovie Carroll

Location: 727 Rt. 323, Penny Pass, AR

In the middle of a story about someone Daddy had seen at the hardware store, he said that the guy was "as happy as a clam," This he stated out of the corner of his mouth, while still chewing pork chop. "What?" I asked. He swallowed and grunted. Me: "Happy as what?" Him: "A clam. I believe I said a clam." Mama smiled at me. I put down my fork. Then Dad caught on. Me: "Why didn't you guys tell me it wasn't clown? All these years, I thought it was 'happy as a clown'." They looked at each other and grinned. Dad said that they'd always thought that clown made more sense. Clams are happy?

Date: Tuesday, May 14

Topic: Without Purses

Category: Action

Author: Ardenia Dovie Carroll

Location: 727 Rt. 323, Penny Pass, AR

Mom: "How do you manage, Ardenia?" Well, in my Bible, textbooks, and novels, I keep a pen and at least two sticks of gum. The gum has three purposes: a placeholder, a mouth freshener, and a boredom buster. In my right shoe, there's a dime for emergency phone calls (except I'm never without a grownup). Since Feb, a quarter for a sanitary napkin is in the toe of my left shoe. Lastly, except for summer when I don't need it and it'd melt anyway, I tuck a lip smackers under my left breast in my bra. Ta-da. I apply it whenever I'm at the sink in the rest room.

Date: Wednesday, May 15

Topic: Proud vs. Pride

Category: People, Feelings

Author: Ardenia Dovie Carroll

Location: 727 Rt. 323, Penny Pass, AR

Pride goeth before a fall. Being proud is being pleased with yourself for something you've accomplished or worked on. You can be proud and still be humble. Pride is a cousin to arrogance. Puffing up and thinking you're better than others. Pride says that <u>one</u> and only one gets to be the best. Proud knows that everyone can feel equally good about something. Proud's cousin is genuine delight. The two often attend big moments of our lives hand in hand. I'm proud to be an "A" student. But there's no need to be arrogant about being the 7th grade salutatorian.

Date: Thursday, May 16

Topic: Cheating

Category: Action

Author: Ardenia Dovie Carroll

Location: 727 Rt. 323, Penny Pass, AR

Last night, I studied for the Social Studies test some more and then turned it over in prayer. I have no problem with Reading, Writing, Math, and even Science. But History and Social Studies I do struggle with. All those names, places, dates. I know things happened chronologically, but I prefer to think of more general terms: past, present, and future. Instead of how <u>far</u> into the past something happened. Today, during the test, I saw a kid glance at dates he'd written in his palm, and something seized in my gut. An honest bad grade is better than a dishonest good grade. But still.

Date: Friday, May 17

Topic: B+

Category: Feelings

Author: Ardenia Dovie Carroll

Location: 727 Rt. 323, Penny Pass, AR

Mr. Mabry graded the tests last night. I held my breath as he passed them out. When I saw my red circled B+, I started breathing again. I couldn't help it so I glanced around and saw a lot of D's. Mr. Mabry said this was the last year he was giving out that test. That each year no one made above a B and his hopes must just be too high on this one. I raised my hand and asked how many years he'd given it. Six. I think we all felt sorry for him. I sure did. Someone asked about extra credit. Instead of answering, he trudged to his desk, shoulders rounded from his burden.

Date: Saturday, May 18

Topic: When I Fall in Love

Category: Action

Author: Ardenia Dovie Carroll

Location: 727 Rt. 323, Penny Pass, AR

They surprised me again today. We were in the car, and Donny Osmond started singing this. I was humming and thinking about his album where he's standing in a field of yellow flowers. Daddy looked at Mama, turned the volume off, and started singing! When I joined in, he started harmonizing. Mama smiled, looked out the window. But then she had to harmonize, too. How did they know it? Daddy scooped up Mama's hand and told me that Nat King Cole recorded it 20 years ago! Mama said, "Remember Jeri Southern's version?" Daddy said, "I do." That tune and all our smiles lingered for miles.

Date: Sunday, May 19

Topic: Trinity

Category: People

Author: Ardenia Dovie Carroll

Location: 727 Rt. 323, Penny Pass, AR

God the Father, God the Son, and God the Holy Ghost. All three are God. I've always kind of thought of them as a really close-knit family, but that's just so I can organize them in my head. How anyone - including God - can be three persons and those three persons be one is beyond me. (Go, God!) Each of them feel very different to me. God the Son is my favorite, God the Holy Ghost is a close second. God the Father I just don't get sometimes and sometimes I don't want to. He can really make me mad, but I keep that to myself.

Date: Monday, May 20

Topic: Cooking

Category: Action

Author: Ardenia Dovie Carroll

Location: 727 Rt. 323, Penny Pass, AR

Mom cooks most every night. Usually there's a leftover or two. She might make meatloaf, mashed potatoes, green beans, bread 'n butter, and a plate full of cucumber slices one night. The next night we might have enchiladas, refried beans and left-over green beans. Sometimes the leftovers don't match at all with what else we're having. Occasionally she freezes the leftovers and then she uses all of those in a soup she drops a ham hock in. Or some crumbled ground beef. Her dinners remind me of the Amish bread starter or the story of the widow whose flour and oil never ran out.

Date: Tuesday, May 21

Topic: What a Friend We Have in Jesus

Category: Feelings, Actions

Author: Ardenia Dovie Carroll

Location: 727 Rt. 323, Penny Pass, AR

Seventh grade will be over before I know it and it's been a good year. Sometimes I wish I were more like other people. I have friends. I am nice. People are nice to me. I get along with teachers. But sometimes I wish I had a close girlfriend. Shep is great. But it's not what I think having a girl-friend would be like. Mama says being the preacher's kid can be hard. That it's kind of like being the preacher's wife. I feel like I'm supposed to be better than other kids. Like I'm always supposed to know and do the right thing. I think I pass this test a lot.

Date: Wednesday, May 22

Topic: Haircut

Category: Thing

Author: Ardenia Dovie Carroll

Location: 727 Rt. 323, Penny Pass, AR

I had my first ever haircut tonight. Well, really it was only a trim. I kept begging Daddy, telling him all about these split ends. I held them up in front of his nose. I tickled his whiskers with them. Finally, he harrumphed and said the woman who fixes Mama's hair could come over after church and TRIM mine. She brought her scissors and I stood on an old sheet. She had to kneel because my hair is so long. I asked her, "Aren't my split ends just terrible?" I think she thought so too, but sometimes folks don't say exactly what they are thinking. She just said, "Mmmm."

Date: Thursday, May 23

Topic: Sunbathing

Category: Action

Author: Ardenia Dovie Carroll

Location: 727 Rt. 323, Penny Pass, AR

Coming home, a few of the older girls sat on the sunny side of the bus and pulled their dresses up so the sun was directly on their thighs and talked about sunbathing over the weekend. (Of course, the boys liked this.) The girls debated Crisco or Johnson's baby oil; morning or afternoon sun; laying on thin sheets or thick towels; reading or daydreaming. Music was unanimous. One girl stated that the sun bakes even when it's cloudy. Flipping every 30 minutes, including their sides, was encouraged. So, I guess there's a 2-hr minimum for equal coverage. I've never considered laying out.

Date: Friday, May 24

Topic: Harmony

Category: People, Action

Author: Ardenia Dovie Carroll

Location: 727 Rt. 323, Penny Pass, AR

Sometimes Mama or Daddy just start singing and the other one will harmonize or become the back-up singer. You might think it would be gospel but you'd be wrong. When Mama sings "Mr. Sandman," Daddy smiles and moves towards her wherever they are. In the house, in the car. And when he starts "Ruby," Mama ceases to move or think. She melts. Eyes closed, she listens to him sing her name, telling her she's like a dream, a song, and twice a flame. I've seen her catch a tear or two. Sometimes his Adam apple looks too big for his throat as he ends in a whisper, "Ruby, it's you."

Date: Saturday, May 25

Topic: Shades of Green

Category: Poetry - Intentional

Author: Ardenia Dovie Carroll

Location: 727 Rt. 323, Penny Pass, AR

I must have known before today
there were many shades of green.
I must have.
But it feels honest to declare
I didn't.
Today, as Saul's scales fell from MY eyes,
I saw Pine, Ash, Elm, and Chinquapin Oak,
Pawpaw, Magnolia, Sarvis, and Sweet Gum.
Each tree was stretching
towards me
And waving a thousand green hands.

Date: Sunday, May 26

Topic: Giving and Receiving

Category: Action

Author: Ardenia Dovie Carroll

Location: 727 Rt. 323, Penny Pass, AR

Sister Ella is 97, I kid you not. She brings tithes on Sun mornings and Wed nights. She lives across the street, and if the weather is "fair 'nough," she walks over. Tithes are a 10th of something. Usually what's brought home on a paycheck. I'm not sure what Sister Ella's formula is. Her latest tithes have been a carrot peeler, a 1938 covered-bridges calendar, a knitted toilet paper holder, a teacup last Wed night, the matching saucer this morning. Mama's smile grows like a sunrise when she sees her approaching and they greet each other like the other one is Jesus.

Date: Monday, May 27

Topic: Cemetery

Category: Place

Author: Ardenia Dovie Carroll

Location: 727 Rt. 323, Penny Pass, AR

Memorial Day is the day set aside to remember people who've passed on. I guess everybody knows someone that's died. After today, the cemeteries will look nice again. Full of fake but vivid and alert flowers that roost on the tombstones and salute anyone who notices. Then the summer sun will bleach the plastic flowers and the wind-tattered ribbons will flap about colorlessly and sadly. Any real flowers brought today will die within days and then, they'll match the bodies beneath them. And we'll all keep marching along to the next holiday.

Date: Tuesday, May 28

Topic: Stupid

Category: Feeling

Author: Ardenia Dovie Carroll

Location: 727 Rt. 323, Penny Pass, AR

It is pure-d stupid. Having school on Tues and Wed before we start summer break! We turned in books last Fri! There were no assignments over the long weekend and there sure weren't any today. Everyone's ornery and today there was a steady stream of kids to and from the Principal's office. Teachers are cranky. And mean. Lots of kids are skipping tomorrow. I thought it made perfect sense but Mom said, "No, not in 7th grade." (What does the grade have anything to do with it?) Shep says our moms just want one more day without us around.

Date: Wednesday, May 29

Topic: Fruit of the Spirit

Category: People

Author: Ardenia Dovie Carroll

Location: 727 Rt. 323, Penny Pass, AR

Why is it Fruit instead of Fruits? Love, Joy, Peace, Long-suffering, Kindness, Goodness, Faithfulness, Gentleness, and Self-control. Tonight Dad asked everyone: Do you have more of one than the others? How much fruit are you growing? Are you at 100%? 60%? 30%? (Well, I'm still grumpy from school so I'd have to answer that altogether I'm at about 7%.) He said: Fruit grows best under favorable conditions: proper minerals, water, air, sunlight, temperature. Well, that sure sounds like summertime to me. I could have gotten a jump-start today. But, no! Mom made me wait.

Date: Thursday, May 30

Topic: Bologna or Baloney

Category: Thing

Author: Ardenia Dovie Carroll

Location: 727 Rt. 323, Penny Pass, AR

Cut from the big red tube at Clark's it's much better than the kind you buy at a grocery store. At Clark's, they ask, "how thick?" and you answer by the space you make between your thumb and finger. They slice it fresh and slap it between two pieces of white bread. If you know to ask, they'll even squirt in some mustard. When you want some to go, they wrap it in white butcher paper and close it with a couple inches of masking tape. They also sell salami with black peppercorns and a disgusting looking pickle loaf with little red things. Dad and I like baloney. A good start to summer!

Date: Friday, May 31

Topic: Dad and the Bathroom

Category: Activity

Author: Ardenia Dovie Carroll

Location: 727 Rt. 323, Penny Pass, AR

After Dad goes to the bathroom, you do not want to go in there. He doesn't believe in using room spray, though he does occasionally light a match. It's a wonder it doesn't blow the house up. Sometimes after he exits, and the smell drifts out behind him, my stomach accidentally lurches. I think Mom's does too. Neither of us offer to go shut the door. Besides, we don't want to hurt his feelings. A lot of times all three of us just try to ignore the smell. Which is hard. Sometimes Mom and I can't help it. If one of us giggles, the other has to, too. If he asks, "What?" We say, "Oh, nothing."

June

1974

Date: Saturday, June 1

Topic: The Candy at Clarks Store

Category: Thing

Author: Ardenia Dovie Carroll

Location: 727 Rt. 323, Penny Pass, AR

Penny Candy <u>looks</u> good and I do like having a little brown paper bag filled to the brim: Fireballs, Zotz, Wonka Gobstoppers, Smarties, Pixy Stix, Laffy Taffys, Lik-m-aid Fun Dip, Pop Rocks, Swedish Fish, Bit-o-Honey, Grapeheads, Lemonheads, Rock Candy, Chiclets, and finally, <u>finally</u> some Tootsie Rolls. But I'm <u>always</u> sorry after buying penny candy because chocolate candy bars are considerably better. A Caravelle "makes your mouth so happy." And "at work, rest, or play, Milky Way." That covers everywhere but church. There, the gum I stick in my Bible will have to do.

Date: Sunday, June 2

Topic: Creation

Category: Thing

Author: Ardenia Dovie Carroll

Location: 727 Rt. 323, Penny Pass, AR

Genesis says the creation of the world and everything in it took place in seven days. It defines day as "the evening and the morning" - not the other way around - but it doesn't say how many hours were in a day. Methuselah lived 969 years. Which is about 900 more years than a lot of people live now. So lots of things have changed. Time is a funny thing, then and now. Hours can seem like minutes, especially when you are having fun. Maybe God just lost track of time. Maybe the first storytellers knew about losing and finding yourself in time.

Date: Monday, June 3

Topic: Dinner

Category: Thing

Author: Ardenia Dovie Carroll

Location: 727 Rt. 323, Penny Pass, AR

Mama's sick today. Daddy said he'd fix dinner. We took her a small glass of 7-Up over ice and some warmed-up canned chicken noodle soup. Daddy fried us some potatoes and bologna and sliced some cheddar cheese off the block. When the potatoes had browned, and were getting good and crispy, he used scissors that I'm sure Mama wouldn't have approved of to snip the bologna slices so they'd lay flat in the pan. He said, "Let's not mess up the table," so we fixed plates right from the stove and sat on the couch to eat. It was pretty good.

Date: Tuesday, June 4

Topic: Tomatoes

Category: Thing

Author: Ardenia Dovie Carroll

Location: 727 Rt. 323, Penny Pass, AR

We start our tomatoes from seed and keep them inside the house until they're sturdy enough to put in the garden. We stagger them so our tomato season is longer. Right now, most of our windowsills are filled with little plants growing in various containers. We water and really baby them now. Because they like to sway in the breeze, every day we ruffle them like they have feathers or turn a fan on them. Once outside, they'll hang on stakes and bloom and grow and offer warm red plump juiciness. They'll work so hard. I love this stage because they are simply happy.

Date: Wednesday, June 5

Topic: A Time for Everything

Category: Feeling, Action

Author: Ardenia Dovie Carroll

Location: 727 Rt. 323, Penny Pass, AR

Ecclesiastes 3. A Time for Everything. Here we learn that there is not only a time for everything but that there's <u>supposed</u> to be a time for everything. Everything. We flow from one thing to its opposite. It's the natural order. We plant and then we harvest and then we will need to plant some more. And maybe something <u>else</u>. We laugh and then we cry and then we laugh again. We start, we stop. We try and then cease trying. We hurt, we heal. The pendulum of time swings back and forth, taking us along. With a rhythm as old as Methuselah.

Date: Thursday, June 6

Topic: Mr. Fox

Category: People (Yes, instead of a Thing)

Author: Ardenia Dovie Carroll

Location: 727 Rt. 323, Penny Pass, AR

Every morning, Mr. Fox trots across the road, trots on past the church, and disappears into the woods out back. His fur is splotched, swirled with charcoal black, walnut shell, and cinnamon. His tail glides behind him like a sail. Sometimes he pauses in his travel and directs his dark eyes to mine. He is soundless. He is clever. He is prompt. (He arrives between 8:15 and 8:30 every morning.) Where does he go? Who, besides me, does he meet? Does he return this way or circle 'round, like the sun seems to? He blends into dried leaves and tree bark and my life.

Date: Friday, June 7

Topic: Summertime!

Category: Thing

Author: Ardenia Dovie Carroll

Location: 727 Rt. 323, Penny Pass, AR

Summertime is wonderful. No hurrying first thing in the morning. No homework. No tests. No combination locks. No bus rides. Time is just slower. And things are easier. Is everyone more relaxed? Or is it just around our house? I like padding around in my nightgown as long as I want. Eating breakfast when I feel like it. Lunch, too. (Dinner is always at 5:30.) Reading a whole book without any interruption! Helping around the house. Getting to things that don't get done often. Like washing windows 'til you can't tell they're even there.

Date: Saturday, June 8

Topic: 5th Period

Category: Things

Author: Ardenia Dovie Carroll

Location: 727 Rt. 323, Penny Pass, AR

It's really an odd thing. These periods. And to think it's all part of God's master plan. This time, I'm going to try to not think about it all so much. Just be matter-of-fact. When I cramp, I'll take Midol, and just go about my business. I know it can be done. Mom does it all of the time. She told me that sometimes women who live in the same household have their periods at the same time. Synchronized periods. I wonder how that happens. I wonder why that happens.

Date: Sunday, June 9

Topic: Sermon on the Mount

Category: Thing, Action

Author: Ardenia Dovie Carroll

Location: 727 Rt. 323, Penny Pass, AR

Jesus begins with all of the "Blessed Be's." Basically, "Blessed are those who seem to be at a disadvantage because, in the end, they will be the triumphant." Can you imagine how the downtrodden felt that day? To hear from such a loving, convincing man that they mattered? That sermon was quite the sermon. He covered everything from being salt, being light, going beyond an eye for an eye, to loving enemies, to ask, seek, and knock, to foolish and wise house builders. He must have preached all day that day. Dad just got through the "Blessed Be's" today.

Date: Monday, June 10

Topic: Glorious

Category: Feeling

Author: Ardenia Dovie Carroll

Location: 727 Rt. 323, Penny Pass, AR

Shep and I had a glorious day. We started at 7 am with bananas and peanut butter. And chocolate milk. Then, we packed up. We took sack lunches, sodas wrapped in foil. Ice-packed glass jars for cold water later. I took a book. He frowned and did not. We rode about three miles out, and called our moms from the house of someone in the church. We hiked, climbed rocks, played tic-tac-toe in the dirt. Rested under trees. Watched squirrels, chipmunks, birds. Tried to imitate them. Shep was better than me at that. There were whole chunks of time we said not a word. Glorious.

Date: Tuesday, June 11

Topic: Sewing

Category: Action

Author: Ardenia Dovie Carroll

Location: 727 Rt. 323, Penny Pass, AR

Mom said, "This is the summer to learn." Well, sewing is for the birds. And Mom. And people who like it. Not me. I don't. Mom said, "It's good for you." and "You need to know how." And "Patience is a virtue." Patience IS a virtue and I prefer to apply it while waiting for Mr. Fox. Or watching berries ripen. Or cookies brown. Sitting at the machine is tiresome and makes me itch. Everywhere. Ripping out a seam so I can do it again! is maddening. Can't she see Shep waiting for me? Can't she smell the honeysuckle patiently holding out its honey?

Date: Wednesday, June 12

Topic: Blessing

Category: Action

Author: Ardenia Dovie Carroll

Location: 727 Rt. 323, Penny Pass, AR

In the story of two fishes and five loaves of bread, Dad emphasizes the miracle aspect. Jesus is teaching a multitude of people who are hungry and probably cranky. The only food around is a boy's lunch. After the boy gives it, Jesus blesses it, and 5000 people are fed. It is a miracle, but what I tend to think about is 1) the lad's lack of greed, and 2) whatever we bring to Jesus is enough. Always. Whatever goes through Jesus gets <u>blessed</u> and becomes more than enough. Whatever it is we give up and let Him have, he'll make it count. Even our transgressions.

Date: Thursday, June 13

Topic: Barefoot

Category: Feeling

Author: Ardenia Dovie Carroll

Location: 727 Rt. 323, Penny Pass, AR

Sometimes people go barefoot so long the bottoms of their feet get thick and can endure rocks, heat, cold. Like they've grown their own shoe soles. I love barefootness just after Spring turns things over to Summer. It's like my feet are creatures that were holed up all winter, started stirring in Spring, and are finally wide awake, demanding to get out. Like Dilly, they want to lay down and stretch out in sunshine. Like woodchucks, they want to rise up and sniff in all directions. Like mice, they want to scrutinize life. All its textures and details and every single color.

Date: Friday, June 14

Topic: Mulberries

Category: Thing

Author: Ardenia Dovie Carroll

Location: 727 Rt. 323, Penny Pass, AR

Long before I see the berries, I see the purple spatters on the road. Mulberries look like smaller versions of blackberries, smaller and slender. They have their own taste though. You could blindfold me and plop one in my mouth and, even if its shape was the same as a blackberry or raspberry, I'd know a mulberry by the taste alone. When they fall from the tree, they take with them the slightest of green stems, which I don't even think about removing before slipping them past my teeth. Mulberries wait on the ground, too many to count, hoping for tasters like me.

Date: Saturday, June 15

Topic: How-to-Sew Patterns

Category: Things

Author: Ardenia Dovie Carroll

Location: 727 Rt. 323, Penny Pass, AR

Simplicity has a whole series for $1.00 each. Pattern 5154 is a jumper with cap sleeves. Rick rack around the bottom, sleeves, and neckline. The bonus: How to work with plaids. I can skip that; I'll choose a solid. Pattern 6508 is a simple (yes!) dress with pockets. The bonus: How to embroider cross stitches (for pocket, sleeve and neckline detail). Won't need that either. Who cares? Pattern 5423 is Sweet Hippie Smock Top. (It's so cute!) Bonus: How to mix fabrics. A lesson on mixing fabrics? Come on! I'll just use my brain.

Date: Sunday, June 16

Topic: Father's Day

Category: People

Author: Ardenia Dovie Carroll

Location: 727 Rt. 323, Penny Pass, AR

Daddy usually preaches about the Father on Father's day and exhorts men to be Godlike. Today, he surprised me. Lots of people don't have a good daddy. When they hear talk of God the Father, they don't want anything to do with Him. To them "father" is a bad word and a bad example. Dad talked quietly today. Pausing to look into eyes. He said God can be the daddy you never had. Even more than the one you always wished for. He said it's sometimes best to refer to Jehovah-Rohi (My Shepherd) rather than El Shaddai (God Almighty.) I liked it.

Date: Monday, June 17

Topic: Shetland Pony Memory

Category: Thing

Author: Ardenia Dovie Carroll

Location: 727 Rt. 323, Penny Pass, AR

Daddy got her because he wanted me to have the experience of riding a horse and Shetlands are small. Short. Stocky. Stout. They're like Basset hounds with bodies too big for their legs. I was 7 when we got her and I imagined being best friends. I'd scoop dry corn out of a large burlap bag in the garage, and take to her. I'd ask her to please be my friend. I'd hold my hand out flat, corn on palm, and hold my breath as her enormous fuzzed lips grazed my skin. Yellow teeth taking yellow corn. She never bit, but she always bucked. I wouldn't give up, so Dad finally did and sold her.

Date: Tuesday, June 18

Topic: Revival

Category: Thing

Author: Ardenia Dovie Carroll

Location: 727 Rt. 323, Penny Pass, AR

A revival is where you go to church every night for several nights in a row or even a whole week. There's usually a guest preacher or preachers who take turns, one per night. It's about the same thing as Sunday nights except there's even more hope that there'll be more souls saved, and more people getting filled with the Holy Ghost. The altar calls can be longer and there can be more imploring people to get right with God. Tears flow freely, and people can shed their old life to be born anew. After a revival, it's important to schedule a baptism. Usually within the next few weeks.

Date: Wednesday, June 19

Topic: Brush Arbor

Category: Thing

Author: Ardenia Dovie Carroll

Location: 727 Rt. 323, Penny Pass, AR

A brush arbor is a revival that takes place outside. Usually in the summer. It's a way of having a revival while staying cooler. Out there in the night air and all. I think it also has to do with drawing attention. Kind of like a spotlight. People can't drive through Penny Pass without slowing way down and looking. It's important to have good music because some folks will pull in just to listen. Not everyone comes into the arbor, some sit in their cars with the windows rolled down, smoking cigarettes, and blowing smoke. Daddy says it's been too long since our last one and that we need one.

Date: Thursday, June 20

Topic: Prissy

Category: Action, Feelings

Author: Ardenia Dovie Carroll

Location: 727 Rt. 323, Penny Pass, AR

You might think prissy is just an adjective for some girls. But I've watched a squirrel that was prissy. He stood off from the rest, full of himself, refusing to play. At church, there are women and men who are prissy. They act as if cleaning the church or mowing the lawn to give Mama and Daddy a break is clearly beneath them. Their collars get tight if they even think someone might ask for their help. They purse their lips and wrinkle their noses and sniff. With self-importance. Daddy knows what I mean. When I ask, he can imitate prissy to a "t".

Date: Friday, June 21

Topic: Skipping Rocks

Category: Action

Author: Ardenia Dovie Carroll

Location: 727 Rt. 323, Penny Pass, AR

Flat stones are best, but it's not impossible to skip one that's odd shaped or round. Right-handed people (like me) stand with their left foot closer to the water and hold the rock with three fingers: thumb, first, and second fingers (Mr. Pointer and Tall Man). They bend their body to the right a bit, and poise their hand so that the stone is horizontal to the surface of the water. They draw their hand back and with a level horizontal sweep and thrust, let it go. Stones just skip on the surface of the water, maybe in a straight line but mostly slightly curved. Sometimes 7, 8, 10 times or more.

Date: Saturday, June 22

Topic: Daddy Sings to Mama (This again, tonight)

Category: Feeling

Author: Ardenia Dovie Carroll

Location: 727 Rt. 323, Penny Pass, AR

(Softly on porch) "Because you come to me with naught save love, and hold my hand and lift mine eyes above, a wider world of hope and joy I see, because you come to me. (Louder) Because you speak to me in accents sweet, I find the roses waking round my feet, and I am led through tears and joy to thee, because you speak to me. (Louder) Because God made thee mine, I'll cherish thee through light and darkness, through all time to be, and pray His love may make our love divine, <u>because God made thee mine</u>." Daddy's ribcage opened wide and the bird of his heart sang into the night.

Date: Sunday, June 23

Topic: Poison Ivy

Category: Thing

Author: Ardenia Dovie Carroll

Location: 727 Rt. 323, Penny Pass, AR

Poison ivy grows on the far side of our house, along with some other stuff. It grows on fence rows, in the woods, etc. I know what it looks like. I also know it can change looks slightly by what it's growing up with. Shep, who is not allergic to poison ivy, came waving it around me like palm branches. He actually said, "Hosanna, Bosanna" as he swiped my neck with it. Obviously, I am allergic to it. I have angry, itchy, weeping, seeping welts and blisters on my neck and arm. He apologized but I turned away. I am not talking to him. At all. Maybe never, ever again.

Date: Monday, June 24

Topic: The 16th Caller

Category: Action

Author: Ardenia Dovie Carroll

Location: 727 Rt. 323, Penny Pass, AR

I've always wanted to see if I could win one of the radio station contests. Today, when they gave the phone number and opened the line, I counted to 23 before I dialed. The first thing I heard was, "You are the 16th caller, please stay on the line." I yelled, "Mom, I won! I won! Turn the radio up so you can hear me!" The two movie passes were supposed to go straight into the trash because we don't go to movies (another sin) but I kept them as a souvenir and as proof. We used the two Dairy Delight coupons for dinner tonight. Mom and I ate for free!

Date: Tuesday, June 25

Topic: Snakes

Category: Things

Author: Ardenia Dovie Carroll

Location: 727 Rt. 323, Penny Pass, AR

Nonpoisonous: King, queen, green, scarlet, brown, black, rat, redbelly, ribbon, racer, corn, flathead, ringneck, hognose, speckled, garter, coachwhip, milk. (The milk and the poisonous Texas coral look alike has red, yellow, and black bands. But: If red touches yellow, it'll kill a fellow.)

Poisonous: Copperheads, water moccasin/cotton mouths, and rattle. Poisonous snakes have wide, flat, triangular heads that are considerably larger than their necks - which don't look different than the rest of their bodies. And, rattlesnakes have that telltale thththth.

Date: Wednesday, June 26

Topic: Snake Handling

Category: Action

Author: Ardenia Dovie Carroll

Location: 727 Rt. 323, Penny Pass, AR

Three kinds. 1) Some churches handle poisonous snakes to prove their faith. It's a special event they all get prayed up for. On top of singing, dancing, and talking in tongues, they handle copperheads and rattlesnakes, giving God the perfect chance to protect them. 2) On Reptile Day, a park ranger brought in specimens. Every boy and a few girls handled a milk snake. Its bright, slender body was one continuous slipping through my hands. 3) I have watched tall summer grass quietly part and caress a long black rat snake as thick as my fist.

Date: Thursday, June 27

Topic: Their Anniversary

Category: Thing, Action

Author: Ardenia Dovie Carroll

Location: 727 Rt. 323, Penny Pass, AR

Mom and Dad got married 19 years ago! Right after Mama graduated high school at 18. He was all grown up at 20. They had a life before me, and sometimes I can imagine it. Tonight, she fried chicken because he loves it. He brought her red roses wrapped in green paper. He sniffed chicken, she snuffled roses. Then she laid them on the table next to her plate. After dinner, I said, "I'll do the dishes." The living room was quiet; they might have been kissing. He sang, "Let Me Call You Sweetheart, I'm in love with you" and she hummed. When I peeked, they were sort of dancing (!)

Date: Friday, June 28

Topic: Cereal

Category: Things

Author: Ardenia Dovie Carroll

Location: 727 Rt. 323, Penny Pass, AR

I bet I'm not the only kid who likes to eat cereal right out of the box. I could eat at least half a box in one day. Over the course of one day. One handful at a time. I'm on a Quisp kick. The little flying saucers made out of corn. The cereals I don't like, right out of the box or in a bowl, are airy puffs of wheat or rice. They just get soggy right away. You can use rice puffs to make crispy marshmallow treats but I don't know of any way to enjoy the wheat puffs. Except just watching them swell up with milk (or water) and fall apart.

Date: Saturday, June 29

Topic: Revival Time at Olive Branch

Category: Thing

Author: Ardenia Dovie Carroll

Location: 727 Rt. 323, Penny Pass, AR

Dad has connected with the traveling family gospel group, "The Singing Powers." Their album, which features their rendition of "Wonder Working Power," has two black and white photos. In one, the mom sits at a portable piano, the dad and teenager guy have strapped on guitars, and a little sister has a tambourine rim. The other picture is of the motor home they travel in, crowned with a sign that announces them everywhere they go. Daddy says they're coming to Olive Branch in August for an old-time revival. We are all so excited! Oh sure, it'll be hot but not as hot as hell.

Date: Sunday, June 30

Topic: Quarterly Card Catalog Update

Category: Thing

Author: Ardenia Dovie Carroll

Location: 727 Rt. 323, Penny Pass, AR

Six months of this card catalog and I am going strong. It's pretty routine but not ho-hum. I'm pretty dependable. I've skipped a few days, and I've also had several 2-card days. I thought I'd write on the bus, or in study hall, to pass time, but when I took out a card, I couldn't take anyone looking over my shoulder. Or asking what I was doing. I wanted to be nice to inquirers, but I had to swallow my reply: "It's for me to know, and you to find out." Mostly because I didn't want them to ever find out. I'm just going to go ahead and fill out the location on all the rest of the cards.

July
1974

Date: Monday, July 1

Topic: Poison Ivy Update

Category: Thing

Author: Ardenia Dovie Carroll

Location: 727 Rt. 323, Penny Pass, AR

If God added it to hell, hell would be worse. The itching has been incessant. (When I heard that word, I knew it was a good word for the poison ivy itch.) You have to be SO careful. If you scratch and get the oil on your fingers or under your nails, and then touch another place, it will spread. Some people say that's impossible. But I'm fairly certain Shep didn't swipe under my arm with it! You have to be careful to not scratch even while you sleep! My arsenal: baking soda baths, vinegar and water, Calamine, ice, bleach water, prayer, and distractions.

Date: Tuesday, July 2

Topic: My First Dress

Category: Thing

Author: Ardenia Dovie Carroll

Location: 727 Rt. 323, Penny Pass, AR

Mom said I had to make something from each of my How-to-Sew patterns this summer. I'm taking them by pattern number, so 5154 was first. I chose solid navy. Cotton. Mom insisted I do some rickrack, too. For "experience". So, white rickrack zig-zags around the cap sleeves and just atop the seam above the bust. Cap sleeves are too short for me to wear to church but it's going to be nice and cool to wear around the house. Since I can't wear shorts. I like it and Mom was right, I am proud. In a good way.

Date: Wednesday, July 3

Topic: Tree Climbing

Category: Action

Author: Ardenia Dovie Carroll

Location: 727 Rt. 323, Penny Pass, AR

I'm a good tree climber and I hope I never lose that skill. The tree invites you and at the same time, it dares you. The first time you meet, you have to size up one another. Look for the best way to get up onto the first branch and then for the best route to go as high as you can. If you pause from climbing and get completely still, you'll feel related. Main trunk, limbs, leaves, you, breeze, bird, nest, sunshine. All members of a big family. Go ahead, wrap your arms around it, close your eyes. Just rest, and you become tree. Swaying and saying yes to life.

Date: Thursday, July 4

Topic: Peaches and Fireworks

Category: Thing

Author: Ardenia Dovie Carroll

Location: 727 Rt. 323, Penny Pass, AR

We buy our peaches by the bushel at an orchard not far from here. Red Havens are the very best. Early Lorings, a close second. They're all so juicy this year that we have to grab a napkin <u>before</u> we take the first bite. Today, we all agreed to have just peaches for lunch. We sat on the porch, hands sticky with sweet juice. Mama splashed warm water on the porch so ants wouldn't come. For dinner, we had hot dogs. Dad lit bottle rockets and Roman candles, and then we all wrote and drew in the dark with sparklers. Then I wrapped them up in orbits of flickering white light.

Date: Friday, July 5

Topic: County Fair and Rodeo

Category: Place

Author: Ardenia Dovie Carroll

Location: 727 Rt. 323, Penny Pass, AR

At the three-night rodeo (Thurs, Fri, and Sat) you can watch barrel racing, breakaway or calf-roping, goat tying, steer wrestling, bronco riding, and silly, dangerous clown stunts. The reigning queen and her court ride each night. Their fringe and hair (and boobs) bobbing up and down. The lights are bright, the dust never settles. Men swagger around with belt buckles as big as these cards and mean metal spurs. Regular old guys and girls don cowboy hats and dream of being on the rodeo circuit, and, because they're so tough, taking all of the accompanying broken bones and hearts in stride.

Date: Friday, July 5

Topic: County Fair and Rodeo, continued.

Category: Place

Author: Ardenia Dovie Carroll

Location: 727 Rt. 323, Penny Pass, AR

I prefer the fair. 4-H students enter livestock hoping for blue ribbons, being happy with red or white, or humbly accepting the lowly brown ones. Women enter cooking contests. Men seem to be the judges for almost everything. The Ferris wheel climbs higher than any building around here. I can see for miles and miles and I'd like to hang out up there. The mechanical bull has a long line of boasting guys of all ages, along with just a few gals. Kids laugh and eat and ride rides and puke. Mounds of stuffed animals wait as prizes. I like the smell of hay and peanuts and sugar and stars.

Date: Saturday, July 6

Topic: My 6th Period

Category: How about "Who Cares?"

Author: Ardenia Dovie Carroll

Location: 727 Rt. 323, Penny Pass, AR

Yippee! My period. Half a year of menstruating. Please, tell me, how does someone do this month in, month out? For decades. The Bible says that the labor of childbirth is woman's curse (Way to go, Eve.) but I think the Bible got this (along with some other stuff) all wrong. I think the curse is this bloating, bloody, blasted period. For almost your whole life. Maybe when I'm ready to have a baby, I'll be grateful for this complicated way of getting one and then, yippee again, I'll get to experience the labor of childbirth which Dad (not Mom) says is agony. What was God thinking?

Date: Sunday, July 7

Topic: ~~Confession~~ ~~Forgiveness~~ Testimony

Category: Action, Feelings

Author: Ardenia Dovie Carroll

Location: 727 Rt. 323, Penny Pass, AR

Brother Gene gave his testimony tonight. He con-
fessed to having sinful thoughts. They were
probably about looking at other women because he
said he had to ask Sister Grace to forgive him,
too. When he stood up to give his testimony, her
jaw locked like a nutcracker. Maybe she hasn't forgiven him yet. While he talked, his face got lighter
and brighter, but hers got red and stayed red.
When they left, he was happy and free, shaking
hands and nodding right and left. She trailed behind
him and didn't look anyone in the eyes. I felt sorry
for her.

Date: Monday, July 8

Topic: My 6th Period

Category: Thing

Author: Ardenia Dovie Carroll

Location: 727 Rt. 323, Penny Pass, AR

I'm drying up for another month. By tomorrow I might be able to wear just panties. Or a little toilet paper folded up. Oh, the luxury: no belt! No pad finagling! No sitting down just right so that I am perfectly balanced on a big old fat maxi pad. Yes, I <u>am</u> a bit sarcastic. Just a tad sour from the last few days. It would probably be better to pray for help with acceptance, grace, and thanksgiving for His master plan, and that I'm a part of it. Though I do think a "mastress" plan would have been a better one. I do hope to be a mama one day. So, maybe I should try to be grateful.

Date: Tuesday, July 9

Topic: In the Sweet

Category: Thing

Author: Ardenia Dovie Carroll

Location: 727 Rt. 323, Penny Pass, AR

"In the sweet . . . by and by. . . we shall meet on that beautiful shore." Daddy hummed and sang this all day long. He must have been thinking of his mama who died in a car crash before I was born. He said she used to sing it a lot so when he sings it, he's probably remembering her. Her singing voice. Tonight, the air was quiet, the stars were blinking, the bats were circling, and Daddy was singing yet again, looking up at the sky. I didn't sing with him but I sat beside him, took his hand, and hummed. At the end of his final "we shall meet on that beautiful shore," his big sigh was an Amen.

Date: Wednesday, July 10

Topic: Bugs

Category: Things

Author: Ardenia Dovie Carroll

Location: 727 Rt. 323, Penny Pass, AR

Fireflies=Lightning Bugs. Roly Polys=Tickle Bugs. I prefer "Lightning Bugs" and "Tickle Bugs." Maybe it's the word "bug" I like. Each summer, we watch for the first lightning bug. Every single glow, all season long, is magical, but the first glow means it's officially summer. Tickle bugs are the very first bug many kids are willing to hold. (We don't say wood lice or sow bugs. That's a science fact I'd like to forget. But that won't happen.) Kids can't help but be tickled as 14 tiny legs tiptoe across their skin and delighted when it curls up, into a perfect segmented gray pearl in their palm.

Date: Thursday, July 11

Topic: Scissortail Flycatchers

Category: Thing, Action

Author: Ardenia Dovie Carroll

Location: 727 Rt. 323, Penny Pass, AR

After dinner, we sat out on the picnic table and watched two scissortail flycatchers swoop and catch bugs. Graceful, beautiful, white headed, with sides that bloom orange-pink. Split tails twice as long as their bodies that serve as brakes and extra wings. Their language is full of k's and e's, crackles and snaps. Daddy and I sat on top of the table and Mama sat between his feet, her arms wrapped around his calves, her hands rested on his shoes. Daddy tried (but failed) to mimic their swoop and talk. He ended up smooching and nestling Mama's neck. They were more like lovebirds.

Date: Friday, July 12

Topic: Blackberries

Category: Poetry - Intentional

Author: Ardenia Dovie Carroll

Location: 727 Rt. 323, Penny Pass, AR

Gravel beneath me, sky above,
    fence rows on either side.
Ball jar in left hand, glove on right,
    hat rim splits my brow.
Butterfly flickers, Flycatcher
    squeaks, Lizard twists,
Grasshopper drones, Mosquito
    charges, Sun scorches.
My feet heat, my eyes seek
    the prize, amid the bramble.
There! And there! Small, dark, sweet constellations.
    Agreeable, flat out friendly. The Blackberry.

Date: Saturday, July 13

Topic: Hair Washing

Category: Activity

Author: Ardenia Dovie Carroll

Location: 727 Rt. 323, Penny Pass, AR

Mama washes her hair every Saturday and in the summer, of course, it's driving her crazy by Wed. I wash mine at least every Sat and Tues night. During the school year, my hair would get oily for some unknown reason. Just out of the blue. When that happened I lightly (important detail here) dusted it with my Jean Nate body powder and let it sit for a few minutes. Then I brushed it all out. It removed the oil and smelled fresh. When I first tried it, I didn't believe that a little dab will do you. So I tried a lot. I looked like George Washington.

Date: Sunday, July 14

Topic: Shooting Stars

Category: Thing

Author: Ardenia Dovie Carroll

Location: 727 Rt. 323, Penny Pass, AR

After church cleared out tonight, Dad and I went for a long drive and chocolate-dipped ice cream cones. It was dark but still hot so the windows had to be down. I'd forgotten my rubber band so I kept pulling strands of hair out of ice cream. As we savored our last crunchy/melty bites, he pulled off the road and shut off the truck. We climbed up into the back and laid on the ribbed floor. The world was dark except for 2 million stars, and quiet, except for Daddy's breathing, and when we both saw the shooting star, Daddy reached for my hand and, with eyes wide open, I made my wish.

Date: Monday, July 15

Topic: The CA Rally Ride

Category: Thing, Action

Author: Ardenia Dovie Carroll

Location: 727 Rt. 323, Penny Pass, AR

The Rally was about 20 miles away. We all met at the church to pile on the bus. Zeke got on first and went all the way to the back seat. When I climbed up, he stood and waved. I felt embarrassed as I moved past seats. People were looking. Smiling, I plopped down beside him. I folded my hands in my lap but his hand tiptoed over to mine. We held hands even during the service (!) and then, all the way back. Our hands got sweaty. I didn't know what to do, but he did. Every little bit, he'd wipe his hand on his jeans and then take my hand again. Our arms and legs were touching the entire time.

Date: Tuesday, July 16

Topic: Zeke

Category: People

Author: Ardenia Dovie Carroll

Location: 727 Rt. 323, Penny Pass, AR

All day I've just thought about Zeke and his strong hands and the way it felt to sit so close to him. Mom and Dad rode the bus, too. She frowned at me once, but I quickly looked away and just ignored her all night. I could feel her trying to get my attention but I didn't want her to ruin anything so I just kept my head pointed the other way. Zeke's taller than me so his shoulder is higher than mine. It was right there, just out of the corner of my eye. I wanted to lay my head over. I also wanted him to put his arm around me. Maybe he'll do that soon. Maybe he'll kiss me soon.

Date: Wednesday, July 17, 9:15 pm

Topic: My First Kiss

Category: People, Action, Feeling, Thing

Author: Ardenia Dovie Carroll

Location: 727 Rt. 323, Penny Pass, AR

Zeke, handsome Zeke, kissed me! Here's what happened: After church, everyone was milling around outside. Lightning bugs were blinking. We were just talking. Flirting. Then, he grabbed my hand and pulled me around to the other side of the bus so no one, except the people driving by on the road, could see us. Then, he smiled, and leaned down and kissed me. His lips were a little dry. A bit rough but I didn't notice until he pulled away. It was as wonderful as I thought it would be. It didn't last long, but lips pressed together is one sensation I'll never forget. I have high, high hopes for more.

Date: Wednesday, July 17, 9:25 pm

Topic: One Summer Night

Category: Poetry – Intentional

Author: Ardenia Dovie Carroll

Location: 727 Rt. 323, Penny Pass, AR

Bats,
black.
Streetlight,
purple.
Moon,
Gold.
Lips,
yours.
Touch,
Ours.
First kiss,
mine.

Date: Thursday, July 18

Topic: BLTCC's

Category: Things

Author: Ardenia Dovie Carroll

Location: 727 Rt. 323, Penny Pass, AR

Question: What could be better than Bacon and
Lettuce and fresh Tomatoes from the garden?
Answer: <u>B</u>acon and <u>L</u>ettuce and fresh <u>T</u>omatoes
from the garden <u>and</u> grated sharp <u>C</u>heddar <u>C</u>heese.

All stacked between two slices of toast,
which are slathered with mayonnaise,
sprinkled with pepper,
and cut in two perfect triangle halves.
Served with soda pop, chips, homemade refrigerator
pickles and a napkin - because you'll need it!

Date: Friday, July 19

Topic: Sweet Hippie Smock Top

Category: Thing

Author: Ardenia Dovie Carroll

Location: 727 Rt. 323, Penny Pass, AR

Pattern 5423 is the Sweet Hippie Smock Top.
With a name like that, who wouldn't like it? I chose
a thin cotton the palest of peach in color with
little blue birds and sweet little birdhouses wrapped in ivy. I didn't want or need pockets. (I was
afraid Mom would insist. She didn't but I think she
will with the next pattern.) This project was
easier than the first. I'm getting used to the
threading of the needle, the thrumming of the
needle, and the throttle (i.e. foot pedal). Anyway,
this top really is sweet and I'm glad Mom made me
do it.

Date: Saturday, July 20

Topic: Parking Meters

Category: Thing

Author: Ardenia Dovie Carroll

Location: 727 Rt. 323, Penny Pass, AR

Parking meters are a way for cities to bring in a little cash and keep people from parking their car in one space and just leaving it. Basically, you pay rent for a temporary parking space. You drop in a few coins (pennies, nickels, dimes) and crank the dial (kind of like a bubble gum machine). A little pointer shows how much time you have. Keep track(!) for when it runs out, a red "EXPIRED" sign pops up for all to see. Merry meter maids walk the square, smiling, chatting, and, all the while, checking meters and tucking tickets under windshield wipers.

Date: Sunday, July 21

Topic: Kindness

Category: Action, Feeling

Author: Ardenia Dovie Carroll

Location: 727 Rt. 323, Penny Pass, AR

As people arrived for church this morning, a big old snapping turtle sat near the yellow line in the middle of the road. Brother Sol set out to help him get across. To do this, he leaned down very slowly. His left hand hovered over the back edge of the turtle's shell and his right hand hovered above the front ridge, just above that wrinkly neck. In one second, he grabbed both handholds and lifted. Woo! That turtle's head shot out like a cannon. He snapped. He clawed. He was heavy! Brother Sol set him down, sprung back, and with his sleeve, wiped the sweat from his forehead. And smiled.

Date: Sunday, July 21

Topic: Zeke

Category: People

Author: Ardenia Dovie Carroll

Location: 727 Rt. 323, Penny Pass, AR

After church tonight, Zeke told me that he's going to his grandparents until school starts. Then he said he was sorry. He could tell I didn't want him going. He reminded me that he goes for a month every summer. I knew that. I was just hoping he wouldn't <u>this</u> summer. He put his arms around me and I put my arms around his waist and we stood like that for a while. I could hear his heart thuh-thump-ing. I felt his chin on the top of my head. He smelled like outside and guy and handsome and maybe like love. I will miss him. My first boyfriend. How can the rest of summer be wonderful?

Date: Monday, July 22

Topic: Crazy

Category: Action, Feeling

Author: Ardenia Dovie Carroll

Location: 727 Rt. 323, Penny Pass, AR

Crazy's been around a long time: Going outside naked. Thinking there are bugs on your skin. Hearing voices through TV antennas. Insisting that things make sense that clearly to others don't. You might think it would be easy to distinguish between confusing behavior and crazy. But you'd be wrong. Take for instance, the case of God, Abraham, and little Isaac. God telling Abraham to sacrifice his own child! And Abraham setting out to do it! One might argue it's just confusing behavior on God and Abraham's parts. But both of them sound like crazy to me.

Date: Tuesday, July 23

Topic: A Month

Category: Feeling

Author: Ardenia Dovie Carroll

Location: 727 Rt. 323, Penny Pass, AR

The rest of the summer is going drag by without Zeke. I miss him already and I really want him to kiss me again. Ideally, kissing every Wed and Sun night would be nice. One month is a long time to be without someone you miss and you love to kiss. I've got good old Shep to hang out with and there's lots we can do. And, there's my sewing. Radio. Books. The Revival is coming up. But I won't even <u>see</u> Zeke until school starts and who knows how things will be then? He may not even like me when he gets back. Wouldn't that be tragic?

Date: Wednesday, July 24

Topic: Watermelon

Category: Poetry – Intentional

Author: Ardenia Dovie Carroll

Location: 727 Rt. 323, Penny Pass, AR

Watermelon green,
Knife silver
Watermelon red,
Seeds raven black
The center of each crescent, a bulls eye
Cheeks wet from that first big bite.
Tongue cold,
Tummy full
Piled rinds on the ground
Everyone's lips all curl up
Shaped like watermelon slices.
An exercise in happiness.

Date: Thursday, July 25

Topic: Metamorphosis Memory

Category: Place, Action, Thing

Author: Ardenia Dovie Carroll

Location: 727 Rt. 323, Penny Pass, AR

I must have been four. We three are at a creek. Daddy holds a red coffee can. Mama has the lid. It has a bunch of holes in it. In the can is water and little dark swimming things. Daddy tells me they are tadpoles. He takes my hand and lowers it into the cold water. I feel the little creatures swimming against my hand. Soft as whispers. I whisper back by wriggling my fingers. He tells me that we're taking them home. We will watch them change into frogs. That they will grow little back legs, then littler front legs. Their tails will shrink. "God's design, Ardenia, God's design."

Date: Friday, July 26

Topic: Hogs

Category: Thing

Author: Ardenia Dovie Carroll

Location: 727 Rt. 323, Penny Pass, AR

I'm glad we don't have a hog this year. (We still have some of the last one in the deep freeze.) Last summer, I knew when the wind slanted north. Hogs, with their mud, poop, pee, and slop, smell awful any time but especially in temperatures of 100 and higher. It is not a smell you want drifting into your bedroom, kitchen, or even in your own bathroom. The sight's pretty bad, too. Flies buzz around their eyes and backsides. Maggots mob the mud. When you pour food or water into their pen, you hope nothing splashes back on you. I always look in their eyes so I always feel sorry for them.

Date: Saturday, July 27

Topic: Banana Splits

Category: Thing

Author: Ardenia Dovie Carroll

Location: 727 Rt. 323, Penny Pass, AR

First, they're delicious. Second, if someone makes me one and think's it's not a banana split unless there's <u>strawberry</u> topping along with caramel and hot fudge, well, they've ruined it. At least for me. Ideally, by the time you're ready to eat it, the hidden banana is cold. (Cold bananas are always better than ones at room temp.) A few hills of smooth vanilla, and maybe chocolate, ice cream rise up in your dish. Caramel and hot fudge rivers run in every direction. Clouds of whip cream are dusted with chopped pecans, cashews, or almonds. Never peanuts and never, ever cherries. Let's dig in!

Date: Sunday, July 28

Topic: The Lord's Supper

Category: Thing

Author: Ardenia Dovie Carroll

Location: 727 Rt. 323, Penny Pass, AR

Also called Communion. 1 Cor. 12:23-29. It happens on the last Sunday of the month. You might not think little cups of grape juice and bits of bread could be dangerous but if you partake and aren't worthy, you are eating and drinking damnation to your soul. And, if you don't partake, others will probably think that your sins are really bad. So, on the night before communion is to be served, search your heart for anything Jesus needs to forgive you for. Pray, go directly to sleep, be on your best behavior the next morning and you can partake without any fear of going to hell.

Date: Monday, July 29

Topic: Challenge

Category: Thing, Action

Author: Ardenia Dovie Carroll

Location: 727 Rt. 323, Penny Pass, AR

A challenge is a way for a person to test something or be tested. Dad says I'm his biggest challenge. I don't mean to be. I just wonder a lot. Sometimes out loud. For instance, Dad says it's a sin to cook on Sunday. But, I challenge, what if cooking makes your heart one big thank you to God? What then? What if you don't consider it work at all, maybe it's just love? And, shouldn't each person define work? Besides, sometimes, people <u>have</u> to labor on Sundays. Cars have to be fixed before Monday morning. Babies won't wait to be born. Maybe challenges, like me, are necessary.

Date: Tuesday, July 30

Topic: Home - Our Front Side

Category: Place

Author: Ardenia Dovie Carroll

Location: 727 Rt. 323, Penny Pass, AR

Some people have bushes or flowers in neat little beds around the front of their homes. Not us. We're busy. No time to plant determined marigolds or tend climbing roses. Though, in summer, we do grow our garden. Dad mows from the gravel church driveway right up to our cement block foundation. On the porch are two rockers and an old short pew, with a long split down the seat. After dinner, we race to the rockers. I love rocking, but so does Mama. I always get up for her. Then, amid their quiet voices, I sit on the steps and watch for star-light star-bright.

Date: Wednesday, July 31

Topic: Home - Our Back Side

Category: Place

Author: Ardenia Dovie Carroll

Location: 727 Rt. 323, Penny Pass, AR

If you stood out back, and faced our home, you'd see: Dilly's dog pen, plywood house, and his food and water bowls; my purple bike with the seat that I've painted yellow (to look like a banana); three windows - Mama's kitchen, Daddy's study, and my bedroom, right in between; a green hose stretching from the faucet to the garden; the wind mobile I made with metal washers, hanging from the shade tree; our old picnic table; the rusted out grill; the shed; seven dandelions, still yellow, and one all ready to blow; a white butter-fly; and tiny wild strawberries at your feet.

August
1974

Date: Thursday, August 1

Topic: Beginning

Category: Thing

Author: Ardenia Dovie Carroll

Location: 727 Rt. 323, Penny Pass, AR

For back to school, I bought yellow Dittos because they are as bright as dandelions. Dittos are great because of the two extra seams on the back that curve up, across, and down the fanny. I debated between yellow, red, white, or black. If I pick up another pair, I'll get black. Because my crocheting is limited to granny squares, I had to <u>buy</u> a cute vest. It's called a "rib tickler." It's dandelion yellow, dark bell pepper red, and collard green. This is my first-day-back-to-school outfit. I think I'm ready for 8th grade. I'll be <u>all</u> ready when Zeke gets back but, for now, I've done all I can do.

Date: Friday, August 2

Topic: A Letter! From Zeke!

Category: Feeling

Author: Ardenia Dovie Carroll

Location: 727 Rt. 323, Penny Pass, AR

Today! I read it three times and then put it under everything in my underwear drawer. He said he misses me. That he's working hard at his grandpa's place. That his muscles are growing. I can't wait to see them! I wrote him back right away. I told him I missed him, too. That Mom is making me sew this summer, and that I'm on my third thing. That the Revival is only 12 days away. That I couldn't wait to see his muscles. I asked if he worked outside without a shirt on. I can't believe I asked him that! Then, before I could change my mind, I sealed the envelope, and licked the stamp. SWAK.

Date: Saturday, August 3

Topic: My 7th Period

Category: Thing

Author: Ardenia Dovie Carroll

Location: 727 Rt. 323, Penny Pass, AR

Well, you'd think I'd get used to it. But I haven't.
At 10am I said, "I wish it weren't so <u>dadgum</u> hot."
Dad said, "The grass is always greener. . ." trailing
off. I shook my head and snorted. I guess he felt
like he had to continue, so he did: "You know, on
the other side." I stared at him. Then, I guess he
felt like he had to explain, "You'll be wanting heat
come winter." I continued to stare at him. I knew
the correlation but I said, "What's that got to do
with the price of tea in China?" and stomped to
the frig, grabbed my frozen washrag, and holding it
to my forehead, stomped all the way to my room.

Date: Sunday, August 4

Topic: My 7th Period. Still.

Category: Thing

Author: Ardenia Dovie Carroll

Location: 727 Rt. 323, Penny Pass, AR

When it's hot like this, I must give off an odor. Everywhere I go. There's no concealing it. I'm surprised people don't back off and give me a wide berth while my Pigpen self straggles my hot stinky body around. My tummy hurts. My head hurts. My privates feel like they're being wrung out. And my pad sticks to my fanny. I'd like to lie down in a bathtub of cool water with a fan blowing. (Like I did when I was little.) But I have to be quick in the tub. Even then, I can end up mopping up blood. Being a woman is making me cranky and disagreeable. And, I fear, smelly.

Date: Monday, August 5

Topic: Building the Brush Arbor

Category: Action

Author: Ardenia Dovie Carroll

Location: 727 Rt. 323, Penny Pass, AR

It is so hot. Dad announces every morning, "It's gonna be a scorcher." We've put it off as long as we can but it's time to get the Brush Arbor ready. So today, he dug holes with his post hole digger and we set the poles in some quick drying concrete. We took a good break and then attached the top cross pieces and covered the whole top with lightweight chicken wire. We'll wait until just before the Revival to stretch green leafy branches across, so they won't dry out too fast. It's a solid structure. And we are worn out.

Date: Tuesday, August 6

Topic: That Kitchen Drawer

Category: Thing

Author: Ardenia Dovie Carroll

Location: 727 Rt. 323, Penny Pass, AR

I've heard them called catch-all drawers or junk drawers. Today I was bored, so Mama made me clean ours out. Scissors, rubber bands, paperclips, pencils, pens, notepads, thumbtacks, scotch tape, painters tape, duct tape, calculator, twisty-ties, a spool of white thread with a bent needle, a ruler, an old pocket knife with two broken blades, folded up sheet music to The Good Old Gospel Ship, a nearly empty blue jar of Vicks vapor rub, two padlocks, nail files, nails, screws, bolts, shredded peanut shells, a very hard caramel, five keys, and, surprise! Our missing ice cream scoop!

Date: Wednesday, August 7

Topic: The Second Dress

Category: Thing

Author: Ardenia Dovie Carroll

Location: 727 Rt. 323, Penny Pass, AR

I finished #6508 today. The sleeves are real sleeves, so I can wear it to church and I did tonight. And, I was right - Mom made me do pockets. The fabric has a black background, but you can barely see the black for all the super bright flowers. Mostly orange, pink, yellow, with a little white, a little lime green. It's fantastic! Some of the church ladies commented on it. Said I'd done a good job. Mama was proud for me. Shep said "Oooh, foxy" but he was teasing me. Later he said, "Your dress _is_ nice" and _that_ was nice.

Date: Thursday, August 8

Topic: From Psalm 59 - 61; King James Version

Category: Poetry - Accidental

Author: Ardenia Dovie Carroll

Location: 727 Rt. 323, Penny Pass, AR

Fighting daily
My soul among lions,
In God I have put my trust.
I will call.
He shall hear my voice
And attend to me.
Wings like a dove,
I fly away.
God is mine
helper.
(If I added just a couple of letters, he could be
my helicopter.)

Date: Friday, August 9

Topic: President Richard Nixon

Category:

Author: Ardenia Dovie Carroll

Location: 727 Rt. 323, Penny Pass, AR

Here, we are focusing on the upcoming revival. However, in other places, people are up in airs about our President. The U.S. Supreme Court fired him so now he has resigned. It has something to do with Watergate which has nothing to do with water or a gate. And that has something to do with an old burglary where someone stole some papers and recordings. There was a smoking gun which wasn't a gun. I think he was fired because he lied and tried to have more power than he should have. By someone's definition. Now, Gerald Ford is President.

Date: Saturday, August 10

Topic: Daddy's Toothpicks

Category: Things

Author: Ardenia Dovie Carroll

Location: 727 Rt. 323, Penny Pass, AR

Daddy's toothpicks are different than the ones Mama gets for company. She offers a small white glass hobnail holder. It matches a pitcher she has and the two living room lamps. Daddy's holder is an old wooden porcupine and his toothpicks are its quills. The porcupine stands at attention on the table next to his recliner. Dad plucks a quill, picks his teeth, sucks and tongues his teeth, spits a bit, and then, to Mama's dismay, returns the quill to the porcupine. Today, with lips pressed flat, she snatched every quill and substituted all new picks. He appeared puzzled, but he winked at me.

Date: Sunday, August 11

Topic: Abortion

Category: Action

Author: Ardenia Dovie Carroll

Location: 727 Rt. 323, Penny Pass, AR

The Bible says it's a sin to kill but if God directly tells you it's ok, then it's ok. Dad says women who choose abortions need to be saved from themselves. That two wrongs don't make a right. What about women who'd give anything to have one? He makes everything sound black and white and oh so clear. But, I challenge: even Bible people seemed to be figuring things out <u>as</u> they lived. <u>Like</u> <u>we</u> <u>do</u>. Maybe we shouldn't automatically think women have done something wrong. Maybe they're just figuring things out as they go. Maybe, just maybe, they're smart and sad and strong and right.

Date: Monday, August 12

Topic: Supper in Penny Pass

Category: Poetry - Intentional

Author: Ardenia Dovie Carroll

Location: 727 Rt. 323, Penny Pass, AR

Yellow squash, green green beans,
two bites of each, no more.
Fried potatoes, cobbed corn, and ham
all please me to the core.
God is great
and God is good.
I sure do thank Him
for this food.
My sweet tea
with lemon slice -
tasty, cold,
and oh so nice.

Date: Tuesday, August 13

Topic: Another Letter from Zeke

Category: Feeling

Author: Ardenia Dovie Carroll

Location: 727 Rt. 323, Penny Pass, AR

He is working outside without a shirt on, growing muscles, and getting suntanned! He must be even more handsome. I started a letter but I'll wait to finish until I can tell him a little bit about the Revival, too. He said his granny makes the best homemade peach ice cream and he wished I could have some. He said when he looks up at the stars, he's wondering if I'm looking up, too. Towards the end, he wrote, "Ardenia, you sure do have soft lips." That makes my tummy tingle every time I read it! He has soft ones, too. Last time he just signed his name. This time he wrote "love, Zeke".

Date: Wednesday, August 14

Topic: Ready!

Category: Feeling

Author: Ardenia Dovie Carroll

Location: 727 Rt. 323, Penny Pass, AR

This morning, Daddy and I climbed over the fence to the wooded area and cut tree branches full of green leaves to pile on top of the Arbor. It looks so good. Then we carried out the folding chairs. Then we drank the fresh lemonade Mama made and Daddy took a nap. Then, we got cleaned up. Now, we are just waiting. Waiting for The Powers to show up. Waiting for the POWER to show up!

Date: Wednesday, August 14

Topic: The Powers

Category: People

Author: Ardenia Dovie Carroll

Location: 727 Rt. 323, Penny Pass, AR

They drove into the parking lot and parked under the streetlight. While the grownups and Babyanna (yes, they call her that!) talked, Jude, the teenager, offered to show me their traveling home. He started at the very back where his parents sleep and said, "Yeah, I can hear Mom and Dad screwing." Politely, I asked, "Screwing what?" He sniggered and continued. Then, at the dining table, he explained that at night it converted to his bed and arched his right eyebrow and then winked. I felt queasy. I turned to go, and he pinched the back of my arm really hard. And then I felt really sick.

Date: Wednesday, August 14

Topic: Night One of the Revival

Category: People

Author: Ardenia Dovie Carroll

Location: 727 Rt. 323, Penny Pass, AR

Daddy asked me to help unfold the folding chairs and then we carried out one of the altars. Several men arrived early to help roll out the piano. Betty Powers sat down and riffled through some songs. Brother Bryar walked around nodding. Babyanna played in the dirt. After I changed my clothes, I looked at the bruise on the back of my arm in the mirror. Mama had already asked what had happened there but I just shrugged. Their singing was ok. Brother Bryar's preaching was ok. I kept rubbing my arm. Once Jude caught me soothing my arm and smiled but it wasn't a real smile.

Date: Thursday, August 15

Topic: Dread

Category: People

Author: Ardenia Dovie Carroll

Location: 727 Rt. 323, Penny Pass, AR

I helped Mama all day. I told her it was too hot to be outside. As I sliced a mountain of strawberries, she told me she'd invited the Powers to come over after the service for strawberry shortcake. I was sorry she had. I kept dreading seeing him at all, and I kept praying. For Jude to be nice, for me to be ok. And nice. He's company. The service went ok. When they came over afterwards, I tried to stay by Mom but after he asked for more pop for the third time, Mom insisted I help him. In the kitchen corner, as I put ice into his glass, he pushed me against the counter and grabbed my breast.

Date: Thursday, August 15

Topic: Ice

Category: Feeling

Author: Ardenia Dovie Carroll

Location: 727 Rt. 323, Penny Pass, AR

I dropped the ice bucket and ice scattered on the floor. He snorted and walked back into the living room. I called out, "Everything's ok. Sorry." I knelt. To pick up ice. I held the last chunk against my forehead. It was cold and numbed the spot it touched. I held it to each cheek. It was quickly melting. And I slipped the rest past my lips. Then, so no one would slip, I mopped up the water with a towel and draped it on the stove. When I went back into the living room, I sat on the floor in front of Daddy's chair. He patted my head and I felt a little better. Jude's smirk mocked me.

Date: Friday, August 16

Topic: Help, help

Category: Feeling

Author: Ardenia Dovie Carroll

Location: 727 Rt. 323, Penny Pass, AR

Today was a reading day. In my room. With the fan on. A wet washrag on my head. Wishing the revival was over, and the Powers were long gone. I'm sorry if I don't care who else gets saved. At the service, he ignored me so I had a chance to watch him. Out of the corner of my eyes. I think he's conceited and rude and as ugly as a possum. I've not been around much meanness but he just might be mean. I think he thinks girls are God's gift to him. He acts like he's a gospel rock star. I don't care if he's ever nice to me. I just hope God will answer my prayer for help and protection.

Date: Friday, August 16

Topic: Spit

Category: Thing, Action

Author: Ardenia Dovie Carroll

Location: 727 Rt. 323, Penny Pass, AR

Yes, it helps us digest our food. But I'm writing about spit because once Brother Bryar starts getting worked up while he's preaching, the spit gathers at the corners of his mouth. White. Bigger, bigger. I can't hear a word he's saying because I'm watching all that spit. Does he forget about the handkerchief he has in his pocket? Does he even have one? Does he have any idea what a distraction his spit is to the Gospel? Am I the only one who wants to stand up and yell, "wipe your mouth, for crying out loud"? He's ugly like his son, who didn't do anything to me tonight. Thank God.

Date: Saturday, August 17 (morning)

Topic: Friday, 11:54 pm – Nightmare

Category: Feeling

Author: Ardenia Dovie Carroll

Location: 727 Rt. 323, Penny Pass, AR

I woke up with such a start! The fan was on, the window open, the cooler night air filled my room. I didn't want be awake because I didn't want to think about Jude the Jerk. My bed is in front of the window. Without getting up I can look out, up at the trees, maybe the moon. So I looked. And there he was. On the other side of the screen. His face was close and distorted. He was breathing fast. And moving his body back and forth. He groaned. I jumped. Then he was gone. My heart was a wild bird needing a nest. I shut my windows, drew the curtains, curled up, waited for morning.

Date: Saturday, August 17 (morning)

Topic: Confused and Scared

Category: Feelings

Author: Ardenia Dovie Carroll

Location: 727 Rt. 323, Penny Pass, AR

I don't know what to do. Pretty is as pretty does. Do unto others. Forgive them that perse-cute you. Turn the other cheek. 70 times 7. Children should be seen and not heard. Why can't I just tell Mama? Or Dad? Why does this feel like a secret that must be kept? What did I do? Today is Saturday. They leave after service tomorrow morning. How can I stay away from him? Shep just called but I lied (Lied!) and told him I was grounded today. For backtalking. I'm afraid if I see him I will have to tell him about last night and then what would happen?

Date: Saturday, August 17 (night)

Topic:

Category:

Author: Ardenia Dovie Carroll

Location: 727 Rt. 323, Penny Pass, AR

If only I could wear pants to church. If only Mama hadn't left that recipe she'd promised someone on the kitchen counter. If only he hadn't seen me leave church. If only he hadn't followed. He was behind me before I realized it. He shut the back door. With both hands shoved me backward against the counter. Unzipped his pants. Pulled out his penis. Hard. Purple like a bruise. Yanked my dress up. Pulled my panties. Covered my mouth. Jabbed at me. Hurt. White goo squirted. Landed on my hair down there. My dress. He rubbed his penis and stuck his wet hand into my private. And left.

Date: Saturday, August 17 (night)

Topic:

Category:

Author: Ardenia Dovie Carroll

Location: 727 Rt. 323, Penny Pass, AR

My face was wet. My throat, so tight. I couldn't breathe. I locked the door. I saw the recipe Mama wanted. I didn't care. I sat in Daddy's chair. I sat on Mama's perch. I went to lay on my bed but the window was open. It was August hot but my fingers were cold. I turned in circles. I wet a washcloth. Spot-washed my dress. I thought, "I'll never wear this again." I said it out loud. I leaned over the toilet and heaved. I splashed my face. My white, white face. I locked the bathroom door. My private burned. Too scared to look. Touch. Quivered until every muscle, every bone, every thought was tired.

Date: Saturday, August 17 (night)

Topic:

Category:

Author: Ardenia Dovie Carroll

Location: 727 Rt. 323, Penny Pass, AR

It's ok to use several cards in one night. It's ok to add to what I've written. Mama and Daddy are home. They seem tired. They're out on the porch and I would be too if the motor home were gone. I will curl on this couch, listen to the ice in their glasses. And the rhythm of their voices: his, deep, hers, soft. Maybe the panic that keeps rising in my throat will go away. And then, I will go get my bath. In just a few minutes. And then, I will kneel by my bed and pray for everyone I know, and for people who are lost and going to hell, and then, I'll pray for me, me, me.

Date: Sunday, August 18

Topic: Sick

Category: Feeling

Author: Ardenia Dovie Carroll

Location: 727 Rt. 323, Penny Pass, AR

I'm sick. I can't go to church this morning. I can't look at food. Mama asked if it was my period. Dad had to ring the bell himself this morning. Can privates bruise? Can they tear like old fabric? Last night when I took my panties off, there were smears of blood. I cried because the water burned. After my bath, I started to rinse my panties in cold water, but instead, I balled them up, wrapped them in newspaper, and shoved them under most of the trash in the kitchen. Love Lifted Me is what they're singing right now. I can hear them. I know the words. Can Love Lift Me? Will it?

Date: Sunday, August 18

Topic: Relief

Category: Feeling

Author: Ardenia Dovie Carroll

Location: 727 Rt. 323, Penny Pass, AR

After church, Shep came over. We talked through the front door screen. I told him, "Don't get close." I don't think it's catchy but still. Finally, the only vehicle left in the parking lot was that stupid motor home. Finally, Brother Bryar and Daddy shook hands; Babyanna and Sister Betty climbed the steps. Finally, Jude (instead of being short for Judah, it should be for Judas, the Jesus traitor) took to the steps. He turned, saluted, two fingers pointing to the screen door where I stood. Finally, he shut the door. Finally, the vehicle rolled away, gravel crackling. I watched until the dust settled.

Date: Monday, August 19

Topic: Damned

Category: Action

Author: Ardenia Dovie Carroll

Location: 727 Rt. 323, Penny Pass, AR

The Powers are gone. PTL. I hope to forget them all as soon as possible. Forgive and forget. All things <u>are</u> possible through Jesus. So, I will keep praying for that. I might pray that he sees the error of his ways so that he can ask for God's forgiveness. Because I think going all over the country and singing about God's love and hurting girls between services is something kin to taking communion when your heart isn't ready. Then again, maybe his soul should be damned. He can just burn in hell. Forever. Zeke got home this evening. He looked over here, but I couldn't go out.

Date: Monday, August 19

Topic: Quiet

Category: Feeling

Author: Ardenia Dovie Carroll

Location: 727 Rt. 323, Penny Pass, AR

My room is quiet. But it's a different quiet. It used to feel quiet and safe. Now, it's the kind of quiet that sets in after something bad happens. I woke up during the night last night. And cried as quietly as I could. Plain as day, I saw his angry penis, his angry face. His whole angry body. How can someone be so angry? Why is someone so angry? The goo just spurted out. I still feel his fat fingernails scrape me inside. Like a chalkboard. Above me, the milky moon was quiet. From the deep quiet, an owl called, "Who, who, who are you?" I could only cry.

Date: Tuesday, August 20

Topic: Howling

Category: Action

Author: Ardenia Dovie Carroll

Location: 727 Rt. 323, Penny Pass, AR

Wolves, coyotes, hound dogs, wind, my heart.

Date: Wednesday, August 21

Topic: First Day of 8th Grade

Category: Thing

Author: Ardenia Dovie Carroll

Location: 727 Rt. 323, Penny Pass, AR

I've got Math, English, Social Studies, Lunch, Science, P.E., Study Hall, and Home Ec. My locker's on the bottom. My combination is 22-8-18. My bus number is the same as last year. The bus parks in the same exact spot, we have the same bus driver. My only new teacher is in Home Ec. I met her last year when the girls went to the 7th grade girl presentation about our bodies and getting periods. Sometime this year, we'll get Sex Ed during Home Ec. The boys get it during Shop. Home Ec and Shop are on opposite ends of the campus. I've made it through the day.

Date: Thursday, August 22

Topic: Sad

Category: Feeling

Author: Ardenia Dovie Carroll

Location: 727 Rt. 323, Penny Pass, AR

Of course, I've seen Zeke. We have the same bus stop. With Shep. Yesterday morning, we three met, all in new clothes. We were all smiling. I tried to figure out if Zeke thought I was different. I couldn't tell. The two of them were clowning around. When we got on the bus, Shep slid into an empty seat and, like last year, I slid in right beside him and scooted over for Zeke but he walked on past and sat in the seat behind us. He patted my shoulder and I still don't know what that meant. He hasn't flirted with me at all. Is it over?

Date: Friday, August 23

Topic: Remembering More

Category: Action

Author: Ardenia Dovie Carroll

Location: 727 Rt. 323, Penny Pass, AR

He called me "Fucking Bitch" when he jabbed his fingers into me. He grabbed Mama's dishtowel to wipe his hand and his penis and he threw it back on our counter. I don't remember, but I must have put it in the hamper because I just checked. It's there. With stiff spots. From that goo? And, his breath. His mouth was open and his stinky breath came in hot streams on my face. He grunted like he was going poop. Besides the bruise on my arm, which is nearly gone, I have two more. On my right breast, and one across my lower back from the kitchen counter, I think.

Date: Saturday, August 24

Topic: Memory

Category: Thing

Author: Ardenia Dovie Carroll

Location: 727 Rt. 323, Penny Pass, AR

A memory is when you remember something that has happened before, or something you've learned. Sometimes remembering is automatic ($2 \times 12 = 24$). Instant. Sometimes remembering takes longer and comes a little bit at a time. Sometimes you have to really try to remember something. Sometimes all of the details just don't come back. Some memories take place only in your head (like times tables) but some memories you can feel in your heart and in your body. It can feel like it's happening all over again.

Date: Sunday, August 25

Topic: Baptism

Category: Thing

Author: Ardenia Dovie Carroll

Location: 727 Rt. 323, Penny Pass, AR

Today we went to Kings River to baptize the newly converted. Women gathered around the female converts (who'd been told to wear dresses, but one didn't) and shielded them from everyone else while Mama knelt and safety-pinned their dresses between their knees so they wouldn't float up when they walked into the water. Then, Dad waded out, said a few words, and invited them and anyone else to join him. At the last minute, I grabbed a pin, pinned my own dress and, without looking at anyone, got in line. Daddy's arms were strong and I cried. I couldn't stop crying.

Date: Monday, August 26

Topic: Regret

Category: Feeling

Author: Ardenia Dovie Carroll

Location: 727 Rt. 323, Penny Pass, AR

Regret is wishing you'd done something different. Like instead of being quiet, screaming out. Instead of being stunned like a deer by unexpected headlights at night, running. Instead of being paralyzed, kicking, slapping, scratching, punching, stomping. Regret can happen right away or it can creep up on you. Even if it creeps up, it will probably take you by surprise. It will seem as if it came out of the blue, and all of sudden, you might feel tardy, or stupid. Regret can make you feel even worse.

Date: Tuesday, August 27

Topic: Burger King

Category: Place

Author: Ardenia Dovie Carroll

Location: 727 Rt. 323, Penny Pass, AR

Living in Penny Pass, there is no Burger King (or McDonalds for that matter) anywhere near. There are in Little Rock and Springfield MO. The commercial, though, is played about every ten minutes in the evenings and the song has set up house in my brain. Like in the brains of every other kid around here. Kids who wouldn't know a Whopper from a Big Mac sing with gusto, "Hold the pickle. . ." I am especially liking the last part about having it your way. I go around just singing, "Have it MY way, have it MY way. Have it MY way, have it MY way."

Date: Wednesday, August 28

Topic: My Way

Category: Action

Author: Ardenia Dovie Carroll

Location: 727 Rt. 323, Penny Pass, AR

My way? I'd bring that creep with his stupid bangs right back here. When he smiled his creepy smile, I'd slap him into Skiddy. If he had the nerve to try his other mean deeds, I'd kick him in his privates so hard, somebody'd have to pull his penis out of his body with BBQ tongs. And I'd tell my daddy so quick and that creep would be so scared, he'd beg God to strike him dead on the spot and send him to hell forever rather than face Daddy. I'd take a hammer to his fat fingers. I'd call him names, like Jerk, and Asshole, and after Daddy got finished with him, Crybaby.

Date: Thursday, August 29

Topic: Fed Up

Category: Action

Author: Ardenia Dovie Carroll

Location: 727 Rt. 323, Penny Pass, AR

Well, I've done it. And Mama and Daddy don't know what to do with me. Today during Math, a boy was teasing another boy who is small, scrawny. Poking him. Calling him Sissy this, Sissy that. First, I just whispered, "That isn't nice." But he didn't stop. Then I said, "That really isn't nice. Please. Stop." But nope. Then I stood up and yelled. "Say it, Say it ONE MORE TIME. I have HAD it. Up to HERE. (Pointing to my neck) The mean boy opened his mouth. To say what, no one will ever know because I flew into him. I ended up in the principal's office and I was NOT sorry. Still not sorry.

Date: Friday, August 30

Topic: Zeke

Category: People

Author: Ardenia Dovie Carroll

Location: 727 Rt. 323, Penny Pass, AR

I never did write Zeke back. Which is awful of me. Every time I look at him I feel guilty and so sad. This afternoon, I sat down beside him on the bus. After the bus started bouncing down the road, I said real quiet, "I'm sorry." Nothing. I said, "I can't even begin to tell you everything I've felt since you wrote. The Revival wasn't what I thought it would be. I've had a lot on my mind. I'm sorry if I hurt your feelings, which I must have done, but I never wanted to hurt you." He took my hand and we rode the whole way to Penny Pass, sad and silent.

Date: Saturday, August 31

Topic: Sleepy

Category: Feeling

Author: Ardenia Dovie Carroll

Location: 727 Rt. 323, Penny Pass, AR

After I cleaned my room and helped Mom around the house, I wanted a nap. I turned on Casey Kasum and the Top 40 and sprawled across my bed. Dozing, I heard the last of the countdown: 15) Night Chicago Died. 13) Nothing from Nothing. 12) Please Come to Boston. 7) Rock Me Gently. 6) Can't Get Enough of Your Love, Babe. 5) Tell Me Something Good. 4) Having My Baby. 3) You and Me Against the World. 2) Leaving It Up to You. 1) I Shot the Sheriff. (I know someone I'd like to shoot.) It must be time for Period #8. I cramped a lot and spotted a little today.

September

1974

Date: Sunday, September 1

Topic: Bells

Category: Thing

Author: Ardenia Dovie Carroll

Location: 727 Rt. 323, Penny Pass, AR

Church bells, jingle bells, tiny bells on toddler shoe-strings so moms always know how far they've toddled off, dinner bells, cow bells (I love those, especially when they are hanging around a cow's neck), bluebells, hand bells, sleigh bells. Church bells. Bell's palsy. One side of the face droops. It's like that side quits doing what the other side does. It's not the whole side of the body, it's just the face. I don't know if it hurts. I think it can be tempo-rary or permanent. Sister Edna has had it for a long time. She asked for healing prayer again tonight.

Date: Monday, September 2

Topic: Me

Category: People

Author: Ardenia Dovie Carroll

Location: 727 Rt. 323, Penny Pass, AR

I've hit someone. I've been to the principal's office. I've lied. Outright and in spirit. I've been disrespectful. Rude. Ugly. Disobedient. Sassy. Gloomy. You'd think I'd be tired of it. That I'd want to snap out of it. I do, but I can't. Today, just before dinner, I went over to the church. I like the quiet and to sit in everyone's favorite pew and think about their stories. I am not alone in being confused. Or feeling sad. Angry. Hurt. Just before I left, I couldn't help it. I pulled on the bell 'til it rung three times. Mama came running and I didn't have an explanation. I still don't know why.

Date: Tuesday, September 3

Topic: My 8th Period

Category: Thing

Author: Ardenia Dovie Carroll

Location: 727 Rt. 323, Penny Pass, AR

I've only bled a tiny bit this time. A spot here. A smear there. I kept waiting for the faucet to turn on. But that doesn't seem to be happening. Did his fat fingers hurt me in there? Is something wrong? And both of my breasts hurt, not just my right breast where he pinched me. Both nipples feel like he pinched them, too. Really hard. And that he did it just a few hours ago instead of 2½ weeks ago. Sometimes just moving my arms across my chest hurts them and my stomach lurches in response. Maybe I'm still getting ready for my period?

Date: Wednesday, September 4

Topic: What's up?

Category: People

Author: Ardenia Dovie Carroll

Location: 727 Rt. 323, Penny Pass, AR

Daddy has asked me, "Ardenia, what's up?" three times since the Revival. I just can't tell him. I can't imagine what words I would use. I can't imagine telling Mama either. I think they both know something isn't right but I don't think they have any idea of what's wrong. They probably think it's something or somebody at school. Especially since I laid into that bully and was taken to the principal's office. I feel like that old snapping turtle Brother Sol got. Even if someone's just wanting to help, I seem to come out fighting.

Date: Thursday, September 5

Topic: More of My Way

Category: Feeling

Author: Ardenia Dovie Carroll

Location: 727 Rt. 323, Penny Pass, AR

I played Monopoly with Mom and Dad tonight. It was her idea. A family game night. That's what she said we needed. She pulled out the popcorn and the 2-liter Pepsi. I think I drew every one of the orange "Go straight to Jail. Do not pass Go, do not collect $200" cards. I kept thinking, "Go straight to hell." Instead of jail. I couldn't help it and I was afraid I was going to blurt it out loud. I'm sure of one thing. If I EVER run into that disgusting donkey ass breath, vile, mean, conceited jerk, I WILL tell him, "Go to hell, Asshole." I think God will understand. I'm sure Jesus would.

Date: Friday, September 6

Topic: Food

Category: Action

Author: Ardenia Dovie Carroll

Location: 727 Rt. 323, Penny Pass, AR

I'm glad tomorrow is Sat because we always go to the grocery store on Sat after Mama's hair appointment. I have a hankering for sunflower seeds still in their salty shells. And Funyuns. I'm going to get the biggest bags I can find. Somehow I've eaten a whole box of soda crackers. Mostly by themselves. But sometimes with a spot of peanut butter, or ¼ slice of ham and cheese on each. Dad says crackers and milk are good together but that sounds horrible. If I think about it, I might vomit. Crackers washed down with orange juice is a good breakfast though, and that's what I've been having.

Date: Saturday, September 7

Topic: HorseSilly

Category: Poetry – Intentional

Author: Ardenia Dovie Carroll

Location: 727 Rt. 323, Penny Pass, AR

Something silly because Dad says I need to lighten up a bit.

Hill Billy still chilly
Near a stack of hay
Will be silly 'til his filly
Gets a snack of neigh.
Frill Jilly, grill Philly
Don't you slack today
A pill for Lily, sweet dill of Millie
Billy lacks pj's.

Date: Sunday, September 8

Topic: Heavy-Laden

Category: Feelings

Author: Ardenia Dovie Carroll

Location: 727 Rt. 323, Penny Pass, AR

"Come unto me, all ye that labour and are heavy laden, and I will give you rest. Take my yoke upon you, and learn of me; for I am meek and lowly in heart and ye shall find rest unto your souls. For my yoke is easy and my burden is light." It sounds like a promise. What happened during the Revival is the heaviest load I've ever carried. I think I'm going to Him. But where's the rest? The ease? The light? Is it possible for someone else to do something to you that unharnesses you from the Lord? I am like the Psalmist crying, "Where are You?"

Date: Monday, September 9

Topic: Presidents

Category: Action

Author: Ardenia Dovie Carroll

Location: 727 Rt. 323, Penny Pass, AR

Only a month ago, Nixon resigned after the Supreme Court fired him. (Shouldn't it be one or the other? Isn't that confusing?) Then Gerald Ford became president. Today he pardoned Nixon for good! Nixon can never be accused of any crime he did or "may have done" while he was president. Unh? It does point toward sin and forgiveness and what usually happens at an altar. But we don't often see it in the rest of the world. People usually have to pay. Even forgiven people end up paying a worldly consequence for their sins. Truth and Consequences.

Date: Tuesday, September 10

Topic: Evil Knievel

Category: People

Author: Ardenia Dovie Carroll

Location: 727 Rt. 323, Penny Pass, AR

Yesterday, Evil Knievel, (why he chose that name, I do not know) attempted to jump the Snake River Canyon in his Skycycle X-2. The skycycle is a vehicle more like a rocket than a motorcycle. Mr. Knievel (I reserve the name Evil for one particular person) is a motorcycle stunt man who might want to stick to motorcycles. This stunt didn't turn out so well. He ended up not too far from where he started but he came through with only minor injuries. I didn't hear what kind. Daddy says his name ought to be Stupid Knupid.

Date: Wednesday, September 11

Topic: Healing

Category: Action

Author: Ardenia Dovie Carroll

Location: 727 Rt. 323, Penny Pass, AR

Healing sometimes happens instantly. Like during or immediately after prayer. Sometimes it takes a bit of time. Like after the flu. Or poison ivy. Even though you've prayed, and believed, some things have to run their course and eventually your body heals. Healing might take a long, long time. Like your heart after someone you love dies or leaves. Sometimes healing never comes. Then, a person might be being asked to trust or be long-suffering. To go ahead and be loving with others anyway. Hurting without any healing can be hard.

Date: Thursday, September 12

Topic: Humor/Laughter

Category: Feeling, Action

Author: Ardenia Dovie Carroll

Location: 727 Rt. 323, Penny Pass, AR

Some people say laughter is the best medicine. It does feel really good to laugh and laugh hard. To laugh so hard that you end up coughing and needing to take big breaths. To laugh so hard your belly hurts and, if you've haven't gone in a while, to nearly pee your pants. Laughter might be good medicine because it distracts you from whatever you are concerned about or what you've been trying to figure out. It's also contagious. There are Bible verses about it. Maybe Daddy should preach on that, or have a comedienne come and hold a laughing revival.

Date: Friday, September 13

Topic: Bits and Pieces

Category: Feeling

Author: Ardenia Dovie Carroll

Location: 727 Rt. 323, Penny Pass, AR

Tomorrow will be one month since the Revival started. Those ugly memories hit me sometimes as hard as my back hit the counter that night. His grimace, that curly hair around his private area, his purple penis, fingernails scraping my insides. Then I feel like I'm falling down a sink hole. Like I've lost touch with anything solid. Parts of me falling and other parts left behind somewhere feet above me. Like I'm not together anymore. I'm surprised that it isn't noticeable on the outside. In a few seconds I come back together and just go on.

Date: Saturday, September 14

Topic: Zeke

Category: People

Author: Ardenia Dovie Carroll

Location: 727 Rt. 323, Penny Pass, AR

Zeke came knocking at the door and when I opened it, he grinned and asked, "Can you come out and
play?" Which was silly. I asked him if he wanted
some pop. We sat out on the porch. Just talked.
About nothing. He slurped his Pepsi and wiped his
mouth off with the back of his hand. He kept
putting ice cubes in his mouth and spitting 'em
back into the glass. I kept looking at his lips. I
wanted to kiss them. I couldn't tell what he wanted. When he stood up to go, he held out his left
hand to take mine - not his right, to shake - and
said, "It's ok. Ok?" What else could I do but nod?

Date: Sunday, September 15

Topic: Anointing My Self

Category: Action

Author: Ardenia Dovie Carroll

Location: 727 Rt. 323, Penny Pass, AR

I've just felt bad since the Revival. A whole lot seems wrong. I seem wrong all of the time. While Mama and Daddy took their Sun afternoon nap, I went next door to the church. Got the bottle of oil from the pulpit shelf. Put a bit on my finger and dabbed my forehead. Then I laid on the altar (You might think that was sacrilegious, but you'd be wrong) and prayed my heart out. The letter F came to mind. I prayed for faith and to forget and forgive and to be fixed and free and feel okay again and to be able to focus on the important things. That or to simply fly away.

Date: Monday, September 16

Topic: Mama's Hope Chest

Category: Thing

Author: Ardenia Dovie Carroll

Location: 727 Rt. 323, Penny Pass, AR

Mama has a cedar hope chest. She had it before she got married. What she saved before then, she's taken out and used. Rather than saving things for days to come, she now saves things for her re-membering days. Today, she opened the chest, and gently rested the lid against the wall. Sighing, she reached in. I saw my homemade Mother's day card from first grade, white baby shoes, one small blanket, three corsages in a tin, a thin scarf, an engraved anklet in an embroidered handkerchief, a small silver tray, a tiny bag of marbles, two bead-ed hair combs, and a tear slip down her face.

Date: Tuesday, September 17

Topic: Hell and Heaven

Category: Place

Author: Ardenia Dovie Carroll

Location: 727 Rt. 323, Penny Pass, AR

I used to think people were either born again or sinners. You made heaven or you didn't, and if you didn't, you'd end up in hell. All sinners lumped together, in a writhing pile of agony. If loving people thought about sinners in hell, they couldn't enjoy heaven. So, while passing through the pearly gates, only momentarily would they think, "Oh, I do wish So-and-so would've listened." Now, I'm thinking there are degrees of sinning and I hope there's a part of hell even hotter for intentional sinners. More hell than just hell. If so, maybe there's a parallel in heaven. A place with even more heaven.

Date: Wednesday, September 18

Topic: Pregnant

Category: People

Author: Ardenia Dovie Carroll

Location: 727 Rt. 323, Penny Pass, AR

There's a Senior at school who's pregnant. She's not married but she wears a guy's class ring around her finger. Looks like a whole spool of thread's been wrapped around the band so it won't fall off. She's very pretty. Her brown hair is long and full. Her belly is round and hard. Her breasts are big. She smiles a lot. Today, we were in the bathroom at the same time. "You look nice," I said, even though I'm only an 8th grader. She said, "Oh. Thanks," rubbing her tummy. "Getting close," and her belly pushed against the sink as she leaned towards the mirror to slip on shiny lip gloss.

Date: Thursday, September 19

Topic: The Radio Flyer

Category: Thing

Author: Ardenia Dovie Carroll

Location: 727 Rt. 323, Penny Pass, AR

It was named to celebrate the first wireless tele-graph and Lindberg's flight across the Atlantic. Here, it's been used to haul stuff as well as me. Mama has pulled me in the wagon many more times than Daddy has. But maybe that's why Daddy's pulling me was so special. I have an early memory. Daddy plops me in the wagon and it's too hot. It burns my legs. I cry. He picks me up and then sets me back down on something made of cloth. The breeze dries my tears. And all is well in the world. Another one: I'm in it surrounded by dirty garden vegetables. We are both laughing.

Date: Friday, September 20

Topic:

Category:

Author: Ardenia Dovie Carroll

Location: 727 Rt. 323, Penny Pass, AR

Date: Saturday, September 21

Topic: Tenderness

Category: Feeling, Action

Author: Ardenia Dovie Carroll

Location: 727 Rt. 323, Penny Pass, AR

Tenderness is when love comes through your hands, or fingers. Even your eyes. Like when I pet Dilly or he licks me. Or when my feelings are hurt and Mama's voice and touch is gentle. Tenderness (outer or inner) can be cherished. You can remember it and feel connected to someone. Another tenderness is when some part of you actually hurts. Like when your skin is tender from a bruise that has a bad memory. Then, if you could, you might wish it away. Tenderness is a spectrum with peace on one end and pain on the other.

Date: Sunday, September 22

Topic: Under His Wing

Category: Place

Author: Ardenia Dovie Carroll

Location: 727 Rt. 323, Penny Pass, AR

I like the image of God gathering me under his wing like a Mama hen. But I'm always reminded of The Little Red Hen. Hen finds a grain of wheat and asks Pig, Cat, and Frog to help her plant it. But they are no help. At harvest time she asks again. They answer no. The same with taking it to the mill, and baking the bread. When the bread is baked and ready to eat, she asks again, and they say yes. But then she says no. Dad says God will turn away and turn over those who don't come to him. That doesn't sound like a mama. Or a shepherd. Or love. To me.

Date: Monday, September 23

Topic: Exhausted

Category: Action

Author: Ardenia Dovie Carroll

Location: 727 Rt. 323, Penny Pass, AR

I know what it's like to work hard. Out in the heat. Sweat running into my eyes. Face red. Breathing hard. Muscles burning. But now I know what's it's like to be exhausted from what's happening on the inside. From feelings and thoughts. Even from praying. So, instead of kneeling and praying beside my bed, I knelt and laid my head on the bed and just whispered, "Uncle, Uncle, Uncle." Over and over. You might think it was sacrilegious, but you'd be wrong. I wasn't calling God 'Uncle'. I was just surrendering. I give. I give in. I give up. I surrender all.

Date: Tuesday, September 24

Topic: Wampyjawed

Category: Feeling

Author: Ardenia Dovie Carroll

Location: 727 Rt. 323, Penny Pass, AR

Discombobulated. Out of whack. Out of balance. Uneven. Crooked. Out of joint. It's what I've been for a while. It's more than that general feeling that the world is not ok. We've known that. It's why we held the revival. Gave people a chance to get right with God before the Rapture. What doesn't add up, at least to me, is the good vs. bad. There were 11 souls saved which is the good. But one girl was really hurt, which is bad. I guess the good wins out overwhelmingly. Was that a price someone had to pay? A sacrifice? How does that fit into God's redemption plan?

Date: Wednesday, September 25

Topic: Crying Out Loud

Category: Feeling

Author: Ardenia Dovie Carroll

Location: 727 Rt. 323, Penny Pass, AR

Shep's mom, Sister Geneva has a favorite expression: For pity's sake. It's different than "what a pity." Which means "that's just too bad" or "how unfortunate." Sister Geneva's "for pity's sake" has an edge to it. When she says it, she flings it out into the space where it hangs like a banner, meaning: "I'm on my last nerve!" or "Enough, already!" At school, I overheard Mr. Barnes say, "for the love of God" but it would have rung truer had he exclaimed, "for the fury of God." When I feel this way, I say, "for crying out loud."

Date: Thursday, September 26

Topic: Fall Fever

Category: Feeling

Author: Ardenia Dovie Carroll

Location: 727 Rt. 323, Penny Pass, AR

I have spring fever in Autumn. It's September, for crying out loud, yet I feel so sleepy. Like Dorothy crossing poppies. I'm foggy-brained like her, too. The bus ride home is perfect for napping, if I can get a window. Shep helps. He gets on first, grabs an empty seat, holds it, and then offers me the window. Wind blows in above me. The engine grumbles and the bus curls around curves. Kids yap and yelp. The sun drapes my skin. Shep's shoulder touches mine and I sink like I weigh 300 lbs. instead of 102. Shep always wakes me as we pass the Penny Pass sign and get close to our stop.

Date: Friday, September 27

Topic: Easy-Peasy No-Touch Fudge

Category: Thing

Author: Ardenia Dovie Carroll

Location: 727 Rt. 323, Penny Pass, AR

In Home Ec, a guest lady demonstrated microwave cooking. Lucky for us, she made Fudge. She wore a lettuce-crisp dress, earrings, mascara, red lipstick, and high heels. She did not take the apron we offered. She set a box of powdered sugar, a stick of butter, cocoa, vanilla, and salt in a fine line. She requested milk. Her red polished fingers unwrapped the butter, fold by fold. Without ever actually touching butter, she dropped it in a bowl. Put the rest of the ingredients in, covered the bowl with wax paper, microwaved for two minutes, and stirred 90 to nothing. Tasty!

Date: Saturday, September 28

Topic: A Discovery

Category: Thing, Feeling

Author: Ardenia Dovie Carroll

Location: 727 Rt. 323, Penny Pass, AR

I watched a spider today for a few hours. She'd spun her web from my bike to the picnic table. I went out to ride but rather than destroy her work, I decided to sit beside her. She had 34 rings of web. Except for the center, the rings were exactly the same distance apart. She traversed her web meticulously, pausing at connecting points, making little repairs. Her body was gold and plump. Her thin legs were about as long as her body. Altogether she was just bigger than a nickel. Her beautiful web glistened in sunlight and I felt calm. Before I left, I thanked her and I meant it.

Date: Sunday, September 29

Topic: Side by Side

Category:

Author: Ardenia Dovie Carroll

Location: 727 Rt. 323, Penny Pass, AR

I've been sitting with Shep or Mom at church. Today and tonight I sat between Shep and Zeke. It was nice sitting close to Zeke. His leg touched mine part of the time. So did Shep's. But when that happens, I always just move my leg away from his. Zeke and I didn't hold hands and we sure didn't kiss afterwards but it sure was nice to touch. It was nice to sing together and share the hymnal. We didn't write notes, or whisper, or giggle, or even look at each other much. We just sat. Side by side and that was enough.

Date: Monday, September 30

Topic: Quarterly Card Catalog Update

Category: Thing

Author: Ardenia Dovie Carroll

Location: 727 Rt. 323, Penny Pass, AR

I never thought a card catalog could be so important. Without it, I would have exploded. Spontaneous Combustion. Mom and Dad would have had to bring in the Stanley Steemer guys to suck up bone and skin and blood and memory and all of these feelings. They'd have been everywhere. All mixed up. Messy. It makes me feel better, to write things down and store it. Save it. I might understand more when I'm older. What I don't get now will be waiting for me then. And we can re-unite and remember and rejoice I made it. It's for me now but I'm also doing it for me then.

October
1974

Date: Tuesday, October 1

Topic: Time Out

Category: Thing

Author: Ardenia Dovie Carroll

Location: 727 Rt. 323, Penny Pass, AR

It can be called in sports. Parents often put misbehaving kids in time out. Mama and Daddy didn't do that with me often. They mostly scolded or spanked. Sometimes they sent me to my room. Which is where I learned that time outs are good for me. I've been taking my own time outs for several years now. Time outs happen by my decision. It's not daydreaming. When I choose to time out, I purposely turn my attention from what's happening outside of me to what's happening inside of me. It can happen on the school bus, the dinner table, or wherever. Time outs are time ins.

Date: Wednesday, October 2

Topic: Blossom

Category: Thing, Action

Author: Ardenia Dovie Carroll

Location: 727 Rt. 323, Penny Pass, AR

Like many words, blossom is a noun and a verb. I think the verb happens first and the result of blossom<u>ing</u> is a blossom. I am blossoming and though I am not the ultimate blossom I will be, I am already a blossom. So I guess they can be simultaneous, too. Blossoming is about emerging, growing, developing (in many ways), becoming, and flourishing. It's thriving in a good and healthy environment. It is also possible to thrive in spite of what is found in the environment. That's about being hardy, persistent, and upbeat. It's a miracle.

Date: Thursday, October 3

Topic: In Case of Fire

Category: Action

Author: Ardenia Dovie Carroll

Location: 727 Rt. 323, Penny Pass, AR

What would I grab? Well, if it were during the night (for some reason this is what I always imagine) and if I could leave my room, I'd grab Mama and Daddy, of course. Otherwise, I'd punch out the screen and run around the house to their bedroom window and scream and scream. My house shoes could help me run faster. Maybe my robe or even my coat if it were cold outside. My Bible. No, Daddy's Bible. Something from inside Mama's hope chest, if I had time. Whatever she'd left on top would have to do. Maybe the book I was reading, if I was really into it. Definitely my card catalog.

Date: Friday, October 4

Topic: Prayer

Category: Action

Author: Ardenia Dovie Carroll

Location: 727 Rt. 323, Penny Pass, AR

After the bus let me off, I went into the church. The side door is unlocked during the day, 'til about 9 pm, when Daddy walks all the way through and then locks it. I sat on a pew. I watched dust motes floating in the sunlight and listened to the silence inside and the cars outside. Then, my heart broke and I started crying. Like I was a little kid. I could barely get my breath. I wasn't praying. I was just squalling. After a bit, my insides started to match the pew silence. I felt like I _had_ prayed. When I left, Mama was standing just outside. "Honey?" she asked but I didn't answer.

Date: Saturday, October 5

Topic: Cooler Weather

Category: Thing

Author: Ardenia Dovie Carroll

Location: 727 Rt. 323, Penny Pass, AR

It's funny. How it just begins to feel like the next season. Besides the cooler temperatures, the air itself feels different. There's something else that you can't quite put your finger on. I've put off grabbing a sweater when I leave the house in the morning but it won't be long before I'll have to wear one. The sun is saying hello from a different place in the sky and it's going down in a different one, too. On the bus, I'm shading my eyes at different times on the route. Sunshine is more yellow, clear skies are even bluer. Am I the only one to feel it? That change is in the air?

Date: Sunday, October 6

Topic: Contradictions and Exceptions

Category: Things

Author: Ardenia Dovie Carroll

Location: 727 Rt. 323, Penny Pass, AR

A contradiction is when a person says one thing and then says the opposite. Or says one thing and does another. Or a situation which demonstrates one thing and also demonstrates the reverse. It's when someone or something is inconsistent. It goes deeper than an exception. To me, God giving the commandment "Do not kill" and telling Abraham to sacrifice his son is a contradiction. An exception would've been giving a commandment to not kill and then saying "<u>except</u> if someone was really hurting your child." The Bible and most people are full of contradictions and exceptions.

Date: Monday, October 7

Topic: Sex Ed

Category: Thing

Author: Ardenia Dovie Carroll

Location: 727 Rt. 323, Penny Pass, AR

Last year, the talk was about ovaries, eggs, fallopian tubes, the uterus (that holds the period or the baby), and the vagina where the periods or baby comes out. This year, the talk was about how babies are made. How the penis and the vagina fit together like puzzle pieces. How the penis gets hard. How it ejaculates semen and in that are the sperms that all race to see if there's an egg they can tag. The first one to tag the egg is It and wins. A baby starts growing and snuggles in for 9 months until its birthday. Was the white goo this summer semen?

Date: Tuesday, October 8

Topic: Puzzle Pieces

Category: Things

Author: Ardenia Dovie Carroll

Location: 727 Rt. 323, Penny Pass, AR

I get that men's and women's lower bodies and private parts fit together like puzzle pieces and when that happens a baby can begin to grow. It's hard to imagine a baby coming <u>out</u> of a vagina but they do, and if that's possible, then I guess a big hard penis can go <u>into</u> one. It would probably really hurt because just his fingers hurt. I know that Jesus started growing in Mary even though she was a virgin and had never had sex. It was a miracle. I wonder if there is any other way, besides sex and miracles, for someone to get pregnant.

Date: Wednesday, October 9

Topic: Sex

Category: Thing, Feeling

Author: Ardenia Dovie Carroll

Location: 727 Rt. 323, Penny Pass, AR

It's weird to think that Mom and Dad have had sex. Probably still do. That the married couples I know have had sex and probably still do. Even when they don't want any more babies. When Zeke kissed me, I just wanted to keep kissing and feel close. I wanted to see his bare chest and muscles and stomach all tanned. So if couples feel like that, they probably really like having sex. That is the opposite of what would have happened if Jude Powers had pushed his penis into me. I hope I can forget that night somehow because I still think I'd like to have a husband someday.

Date: Thursday, October 10

Topic: A Scare

Category: Feelings

Author: Ardenia Dovie Carroll

Location: 727 Rt. 323, Penny Pass, AR

When I got home from school, I opened the back door like I always do and yelled, "I'm home" like I always do but Mama didn't answer like she always does. I hollered again. Nobody was home. Our car and pickup were in the driveway. The church door was closed and locked. Had the Rapture taken place? Was I more sinful than I thought? Nobody had disappeared on the bus so either we were all bad off or maybe it happened between the bus and the back door. Then, across the street, Sister Ella's screen door slammed and Mom and Dad appeared. Sighing with relief, I smiled and waved.

Date: Friday, October 11

Topic: Swears, Promises, and Vows

Category: Things

Author: Ardenia Dovie Carroll

Location: 727 Rt. 323, Penny Pass, AR

Promising and swearing are different. The Bible says to not swear. Don't swear by heaven, because it's God's throne. Or by earth - it's His footstool. Neither by our heads, hearts, or lives, because we don't have any control over anything. No cross-my-heart-and-hope-to-die's to demonstrate that what we're saying is truth and that we are being sincere. Our promises must be good enough and it's important to be true to our word. That's integrity. Vows (like wedding vows) are a step up from promises; more serious and more binding. They stand no matter what.

Date: Saturday, October 12

Topic: Sleeping Like a Baby

Category: Action

Author: Ardenia Dovie Carroll

Location: 727 Rt. 323, Penny Pass, AR

I hadn't done this in a long time. Last night, when I woke up in the middle of the night, I crept into Mama and Daddy's bedroom. Holding my breath, I watched their still but for breathing bodies. Listened to air winding through their noses. Finally taking a breath of my own, I went to Mama's side and touched her arm. She barely woke, and, like when I was little, she scooched towards the middle and drew me in and tucked me in under her wing. Daddy shifted. While Mama's breath grazed the top of my head, I fell back to sleep. When I woke up, the room had light and they were both gone.

Date: Sunday, October 13

Topic: Are All Things Possible?

Category: Feelings

Author: Ardenia Dovie Carroll

Location: 727 Rt. 323, Penny Pass, AR

Is it possible to believe in God and talk about God without ever using the word God? Is it possible that God is even more than what we learn about? That we just got one side of a multi-sided story? Is it possible that Jesus is Savior to people who feel about "something" the way I feel about Him? Is it possible to have God's love inside of you without giving Him credit for it? Or, would that be another kind of love? Is it possible to give your heart and life to God in a way other than the way we do? In Matthew, Jesus says that with God, all things are possible.

Date: Monday, October 14

Topic: Back Door

Category: Place

Author: Ardenia Dovie Carroll

Location: 727 Rt. 323, Penny Pass, AR

After school, in Winter, open our back door and what do you smell? Soup or Stew or Roast or Chili. Apple cake or Chocolate Chip Cookies or some kind of pie. The heat from the furnace in the living room. And Mom. In late Spring? Mr. Clean. Windex. Outdoors. (Why does the outdoors inside smell different from the outdoors outside?) Cucumbers and tomatoes can scent up a room entirely and that's what opening our back door in Summer smells like. But right now, in Fall? Banana bread, pumpkin bread, apple butter. And Mom. The colder it gets, the more Mom there is.

Date: Tuesday, October 15

Topic: Bigger Breasts

Category: Things

Author: Ardenia Dovie Carroll

Location: 727 Rt. 323, Penny Pass, AR

I came home so tired, I had to rest before I could do anything else. Even before getting my snack. When I lie on my stomach my breasts hurt. Actually, they hurt a lot of the time and they're getting bigger. Maybe I'm having growing pains like I got in my legs when I was six. If this keeps up, I'll have to get some new bras. And my stomach, maybe it's just nerves, but I feel queasy whenever I think about the Revival and that's the very first thing I think of when I wake up every morning. Saltines help a little. I just grab a few as I head out the door to the bus stop.

Date: Wednesday, October 16

Topic: Respect

Category: Action

Author: Ardenia Dovie Carroll

Location: 727 Rt. 323, Penny Pass, AR

One reason I love Jesus so much is that He was respectful. Wherever He went, He respected people. Who they were, where they were in their lives, all while He was welcoming them into his fold. I think He also respected animals, birds, fish, dirt, really all of nature. He must have spent time watching what happens out in nature, among all of God's created. And he loved it all, too, because that's what he used in his parables. His love was so deep that everyone and everything already had a place in his human heart, so respect was effort- less.

Date: Thursday, October 17

Topic: Power

Category: Thing

Author: Ardenia Dovie Carroll

Location: 727 Rt. 323, Penny Pass, AR

There's physical power. Daddy will always have more of that than Mama or me. There's mental power - the ability to really focus and stick with something. Mom has more than me and probably more than Dad. Spiritual power comes from God, and to have it, one must be a vessel. So it isn't really yours. Also, there's the power where someone, somehow, gets others to do something. There's the power when someone takes whatever they want without considering others. There's emotional power. I'd say that's the ability to withstand inner pain. Being durable. I'm pretty good at that.

Date: Friday, October 18

Topic: Oh, Zeke

Category:

Author: Ardenia Dovie Carroll

Location: 727 Rt. 323, Penny Pass, AR

I saw Zeke at the lockers today, smiling his smile at LouAnna Gray. She's so pretty. Blond hair. Blue eyes. Opposite of me. Her face reminds me of Mary Ingalls but LouAnna has shinier hair. I looked away but then I looked back and watched. I felt sad; he looked happy. I didn't feel mad or jealous. I just hurt like I always do when I see him. Then he saw me, glanced away, but then he looked right back. I smiled halfway and nodded and he smiled halfway and nodded and LouAnna looked over her shoulder towards me. I turned my head, shut my locker, and walked the other way. Oh, Zeke.

Date: Saturday, October 19

Topic: Firewood

Category: Thing, Action

Author: Ardenia Dovie Carroll

Location: 727 Rt. 323, Penny Pass, AR

I helped Dad all day. Every fall, he helps an elderly lady in the church. She's a widow. Her house is heated by an outside furnace that she loads with firewood. It's hard on her; that furnace is 20 feet from the house. Several days ago, Dad cut down some trees on her property. Those are for next year. Today, we cut up the trees he took down last year, hauled the chunks to the house, split them in her husband's splitter, and stacked the wood nice and neat for her. For lunch, she invited us in for chili. It was invigorating to work outside. Gloves and boots and fresh air and Daddy all day.

Date: Sunday, October 20

Topic: Suffering

Category: Feeling, Thing

Author: Ardenia Dovie Carroll

Location: 727 Rt. 323, Penny Pass, AR

King David had some low points. Crying out from the depths of his despair. Where are you, Lord? Job suffered boils, his wealth vanished, livestock died, his children died. All he had left were his wife who told him to curse God and die, and friends who told him he must have done something to deserve his suffering. He didn't know it, but God let Satan torment him. (Another thing that I don't get.) Neither David nor Job could DO anything about their situation. Praying didn't help a thing. One day, I guess things just began to look up. I think they were changed forever by suffering.

Date: Monday, October 21

Topic:

Category:

Author: Ardenia Dovie Carroll

Location: 727 Rt. 323, Penny Pass, AR

Date: Tuesday, October 22

Topic: Blood, Blood, Blood

Category:

Author: Ardenia Dovie Carroll

Location: 727 Rt. 323, Penny Pass, AR

Yesterday, I woke up feeling blood gush out. I could barely run to the bathroom, it hurt so <u>bad</u>. I sat on the commode and blood poured out. I thought of the woman with the issue of blood; if I could but touch the hem of His garment. I knew there had to be blood on the bed. I could see it on the floor. I smudged the puddles I could reach with toilet paper. Knives jabbed into my sides and down to my bottom. I was really scared but I only cried a little. It was hard to be quiet. I leaned over and hugged my knees. My legs were shaking. I was sweating and cold. Then Mama's alarm went off.

Date: Tuesday, October 22

Topic: My 9th Period

Category:

Author: Ardenia Dovie Carroll

Location: 727 Rt. 323, Penny Pass, AR

I heard her old slippers scruff across the floor and stop at the bathroom. "Ardenia?" "Mama, I started my period and it's really, really bad. There's blood in the bed. Sorry, Mama." Mama was quiet. I heard her walk into my room. After a minute she was back. "Sweetie, I've pulled the sheets and I'm gonna sponge off the mattress. Do you need anything?" I told her I didn't think so but that my cramps were so bad I didn't think I could get up. She said Dad could pee outside this morning and to take my time. So I did. From the crack under the door, I saw her shadow as she wiped the floor.

Date: Tuesday, October 22

Topic: Flu, too?

Category:

Author: Ardenia Dovie Carroll

Location: 727 Rt. 323, Penny Pass, AR

My belly hurt so bad, I was sweating, and I felt like I could throw up. I stretched to the faucet, turned on the cold water, and put a little on my face. Maybe it was the flu and my period? Mama checked on me again. "Ardenia, what's going on?" I told her maybe it was the flu, too. I laid my face on the counter and took a tiny nap. Fierce cramps woke me. I moaned. Felt something in my vagina. Heard a plop in the toilet. I was scared to look. "Ardenia, let me in." "Mama, I can't get up." She must have pulled one of her bobby pins. As she fiddled with the lock, I flushed.

Date: Tuesday, October 22

Topic:

Category:

Author: Ardenia Dovie Carroll

Location: 727 Rt. 323, Penny Pass, AR

She opened the door. "Honey?" I told her I didn't know but this was really bad. I told her that my last period hadn't been hardly anything at all and I hadn't had any cramps either. Maybe this time I'm making up for it? She checked my head for fever. She knelt in front of me and fingercombed my wet hair away from my face. Her eyebrows huddled together. She placed her hands on my wobbling knees and patted. "You've sat here so long, your legs aren't getting enough circulation. Let's get you to bed." She got my belt and a super Kotex. A warm washcloth. I told her I didn't need help.

Date: Tuesday, October 22

Topic:

Category:

Author: Ardenia Dovie Carroll

Location: 727 Rt. 323, Penny Pass, AR

She said, "I'll step outside but the door stays unlocked, Ardenia Dovie." I could barely stand but I did. The warm washcloth felt good. I felt light headed but I wrangled everything into place. In the turquoise toilet bowl the water was tomato red. In the mirror my face was as pale as the Ivory soap. I started to rinse out the washcloth in the sink but Mama said, "I'll get that." I flushed again. She inched open the door and held out her hand. As she walked me to bed, I asked where Daddy was. "Oh, he's somewhere outside. He left the house to just us women this morning."

Date: Tuesday, October 22

Topic: More Blood

Category:

Author: Ardenia Dovie Carroll

Location: 727 Rt. 323, Penny Pass, AR

Mama had made my bed and placed a towel underneath the sheet and one on top. I placed my bottom in the middle of the towels, and folded another one to put between my legs and fell asleep. I slept for hours. Cramps woke me from time to time but they weren't nearly as bad. I did not want to move when I woke up because I didn't want to set them off again. Mama came to check on me, and asked "chicken noodle or tomato?" I thought of the toilet earlier and told her chicken noodle. When she brought the cup, I sat up, and felt another gush. The soup had to wait.

Date: Tuesday, October 22

Topic: Yesterday, Today, Tomorrow

Category:

Author: Ardenia Dovie Carroll

Location: 727 Rt. 323, Penny Pass, AR

I stayed in bed all day yesterday except for going to the bathroom to change pads. Which I did often. I flowed heavy and my whole body was tired. Today, I still hurt where I think my womb is. Mama keeps humming and offering to rub my back. And, even though I don't want to, I keep thinking about that night. The white goo spurting out of the end of his penis, his wet hand, his hard fingernails, my scraped vagina. Something tells me that yesterday and that night are connected but I don't get it. Tomorrow I hope to go to school and apply my brain to things that add up and make sense.

Date: Wednesday, October 23

Topic: Milkshake

Category: Thing

Author: Ardenia Dovie Carroll

Location: 727 Rt. 323, Penny Pass, AR

I've been ready to drop since the Revival. I've been so tired, sleepy, and weary. Today was even worse. I can honestly say, "I feel like I've been run over by a Mack truck." There's not a single place I don't hurt. I made it to school but I called home at 10 to see if Daddy could come and get me. I fell asleep in the car when he stopped at the hardware store. By then it was nearly lunch time. He offered to take me out for lunch. I told him I didn't think I could sit up at the table. We got chocolate milkshakes at the drive-through. It was so, so good. That and the sunshine in the car.

Date: Thursday, October 24

Topic: Touching Stars

Category: Feeling, Action

Author: Ardenia Dovie Carroll

Location: 727 Rt. 323, Penny Pass, AR

This morning Mama said, "Why don't you just stay home another day, Ardenia?" She didn't have to ask twice. I changed my pad and fell right back to sleep. I got up about noon. Wore my pajamas all day. I sat out on the front porch with Touching Stars wrapped around me and kept moving so I stayed in the sun. Mom brought me hot tea with honey and told me she was a bit worried about me and I said, "join the crowd." I didn't mean to be sarcastic. I think she knew that because all she did for about ten minutes was comb my hair with her fingers.

Date: Friday, October 25

Topic: Missing Another Day

Category: Feeling

Author: Ardenia Dovie Carroll

Location: 727 Rt. 323, Penny Pass, AR

Why not miss a whole week? What's another day? Mom called the school and asked if my teachers could send homework assignments back with Shep. I called Shep before he left for school to give him my locker combination. If I can trust anybody with that, it's him. I'll take it easy one more day. My body begs to curl up on its side, with my knees almost to my chest. Everything just wants to sleep. Some more. A bit more. That's today. Then I'll try to get caught up before Monday. What's the saying? "I feel spent"? Emptied out. Hollowed out.

Date: Saturday, October 26

Topic: Homework

Category: Things

Author: Ardenia Dovie Carroll

Location: 727 Rt. 323, Penny Pass, AR

I've spent all day doing homework and I'm just about finished. Tomorrow I need to do some reading but all of the written stuff is done. I think I'll be ready for Monday. I'll put this week behind me and hope I never have another period like this again. I can't miss that much school!

Date: Sunday, October 27

Topic: Autumn Leaves

Category: Action

Author: Ardenia Dovie Carroll

Location: 727 Rt. 323, Penny Pass, AR

If you think of leaves as a verb instead of a noun, you can picture Autumn leaving. For Winter. It's more of a movie than a story that way. Rose red, dandelion yellow, marigold orange, and potato brown all swirling to the ground to settle in as Winter's quiet quilt. Meanwhile, trees stand barer and barer to the wind, bare for the world, and this year, bare, with me.

Date: Monday, October 28

Topic: Breasts

Category: Things

Author: Ardenia Dovie Carroll

Location: 727 Rt. 323, Penny Pass, AR

The bumpy bus ride in this morning felt like an old friend. Familiar in every way. Shep could tell I wanted to be quiet. We just bounced along. Both of us trying to ignore my breasts when the bouncing was especially big. It can be so embarrassing! Sometimes, I just cross my arms to hold them in place. Some girls with big breasts flaunt them by sitting up straight. As if daring the guys to look and then daring them to try to look the other way. Other girls wear loose tops, slump over, and curl their shoulders inward to try to hide them.

Date: Tuesday, October 29

Topic: Coloring

Category: Action

Author: Ardenia Dovie Carroll

Location: 727 Rt. 323, Penny Pass, AR

Mama and I used to color all of the time. At the kitchen table. Cuddling on the couch. Sitting in the floor. We haven't colored in long, long time. After dinner tonight, she came into my room carrying a stack of old coloring books and the tub of crayons. Both eyebrows were raised with her question. First, I thought I didn't want to, but second, I realized I did. I nodded and moved to get up but she came smiling and shaking her head and settled into the center of the bed with me. It was nice. The waxy rub against paper. Our fingers riffling color. Just Mama and me.

Date: Wednesday, October 30

Topic: Halloween

Category: Thing

Author: Ardenia Dovie Carroll

Location: 727 Rt. 323, Penny Pass, AR

October is almost over. Halloween is tomorrow. We don't do much for it. There'll be a bowl of candy by the front door. We'll turn the porch light on to be welcoming. If it's nice enough, we'll sit outside. We'll definitely sip apple cider and Shep will probably come over to hang out. I haven't dressed up or gone trick or treating in years. Dad doesn't like the ghost and goblin focus. Mama dislikes that the way people dress up scares the little ones. She says it's the worst day of the year for them and then they get laughed at for being scared.

Date: Thursday, October 31

Topic: Boxing

Category: Action

Author: Ardenia Dovie Carroll

Location: 727 Rt. 323, Penny Pass, AR

Fighting is wrong but it is also a sport. One that Dad likes to watch. The Rumble in the Jungle with Muhammad Ali (32) and George Foreman (25) was a match he wanted to see and would have happily stayed up late to watch it. It was televised by closed circuit TV at 425 US locations, but Penny Pass wasn't one of them. Daddy got the paper today and read every word twice. Quickly, to himself; then aloud, with feeling. Ali won by a knock out with only 2 seconds left in Round 8. Foreman "fell to the canvas like a tree." Daddy said it's a crying shame it wasn't televised for everyone.

November

1974

Date: Friday, November 1

Topic: Connected

Category: Feeling

Author: Ardenia Dovie Carroll

Location: 727 Rt. 323, Penny Pass, AR

Soon it will be Thanksgiving, and then, Christmas. Sometimes my heart feels wide open. Like it's waiting to be connected to another. Another heart, another person, place, or thing. Today, that happened in the cafeteria. I noticed the scrawny pine outside, his branches, the way the wind rippled through. He became lovely before my eyes. A drab cardinal thought so, too, because she dropped into the pine and wrapped claws around a branch. I stopped chewing to better feel her claw and warm pulsing body, his fragrant branch, and the living wind.

Date: Saturday, November 2

Topic: Pleasure

Category: Feeling

Author: Ardenia Dovie Carroll

Location: 727 Rt. 323, Penny Pass, AR

On Saturdays, when we go for groceries, Daddy half-fills a Brach's white and pink sack with candy. Assorted caramels, hard butterscotch and peppermints, and chocolate-covered creams. After church on Sunday, he and Mama stand at the back door, shaking hands with everyone. Holding the sack in his left hand, he shakes and then, with a big smile, reaches in. Sometimes, though, he peers in first, to specially pick for the person before him. The old ones with few or no teeth can't chew caramels and the young ones could choke on hard discs. <u>And</u> because he loves each and every one.

Date: Sunday, November 3

Topic: Red and Yellow, Black and White

Category: Action

Author: Ardenia Dovie Carroll

Location: 727 Rt. 323, Penny Pass, AR

Daddy began his sermon this morning by singing, "Jesus loves the little children, all the children of the world." He sang it once, looked around, and started again. People looked at each other, trying to figure out what he was doing, and if they were supposed to be doing something other than listening. When he started the third time, a toddler wiggled into the aisle and started singing, too. She twirled and danced with her arms fluttering. Daddy picked her up and they waltzed and sang up one aisle and down another. By then we were all singing and feeling precious.

Date: Sunday, November 3

Topic: They are Precious in His Sight

Category: Feeling

Author: Ardenia Dovie Carroll

Location: 727 Rt. 323, Penny Pass, AR

When a person <u>feels</u> precious, it's easy to see how God sees others as precious, too. It's not like there's a shortage. It's always there; we just forget how precious we are to God. This morning, after the song, Daddy said he could just ask someone to pray us out because after that, a sermon wasn't needed. Somebody hollered out, "Amen, Brother Collie!" Daddy grinned, shook his head. Then he got real still. Cocked his head like he was listening. Then he nodded and said, "Ok." We dismissed 30 minutes early but nobody left. We were all too busy being precious together.

Date: Monday, November 4

Topic: Precious, continued.

Category: Feeling, Action

Author: Ardenia Dovie Carroll

Location: 727 Rt. 323, Penny Pass, AR

Feeling precious has been a great way to start the week. I was looking for precious people all day and I found them everywhere! My bus driver who smiles at every kid who climbs on. Even the ornery ones. The janitor joking as he pushes his mop bucket through the cafeteria. The lunch ladies elbowing one another and giggling. Couples holding hands. The guy who tossed his bread crumbs out for the squirrel who then inched up and ate them right then and there. Shep. Zeke. Mama who hugs me at the door. Daddy who sings his way into my heart.

Date: Tuesday, November 5

Topic: Dilly Dally

Category: Person!

Author: Ardenia Dovie Carroll

Location: 727 Rt. 323, Penny Pass, AR

Dilly is a good dog. He only barks when it's important so he's not in trouble very often. He's a beagle with typical markings: black back, white underside, white legs. His head is a warm plop of caramel, except for that heart-shaped pond of pure white on the very top which then turns into a thin creak and runs down between his eyes nearly all the way to his wet nose. His ears feel like the plant called lambs ears. Velvety. Softer than peach fuzz. He asks questions by cocking his head to the left. He sighs. He loves ice cream and bones and overripe bananas and me.

Date: Wednesday, November 6

Topic: Weak

Category: Feeling

Author: Ardenia Dovie Carroll

Location: 727 Rt. 323, Penny Pass, AR

We might think of weakness as a weakness. A 'less than' of some sort. Something that gets in the way of what we want or need to be or do. Paul had a thorn in the flesh - a weakness. I guess everyone does. Some people just hide theirs better. Whatever they are, we are told that God's power is made perfect through our weaknesses. If we look at it this way, rather than being something we want to be rid of, we can see them as good opportunities for God to do what God does. I feel weak all over, so I am a great place for God to work.

Date: Thursday, November 7

Topic: Two for Tea

Category: Thing

Author: Ardenia Dovie Carroll

Location: 727 Rt. 323, Penny Pass, AR

We all like sweet ice tea in the summer. When it gets cold outside, Mom and I like hot tea with honey and sometimes a small squirt of lemon juice. I filled our avocado green kettle and put it on the stove. When it whistled, we both went and stood side by side. We each placed a little bag in our favorite mugs, ladled honey from the honey pot we've had for as long as I can remember, poured the steaming water, covered with a saucer, and waited. Mama put a handful of Fig Newtons on a plate. Then we sat, just the two of us, at the table. Tea for two.

Date: Friday, November 8

Topic: My Something Lost Dream

Category: Thing, Feeling

Author: Ardenia Dovie Carroll

Location: 727 Rt. 323, Penny Pass, AR

In the dream, I'm checking my bed for something I've lost. In the dark, my hands scramble under the covers. Down to the very corners where the sheet is tucked so tightly that my fingers are flattened. Not there. My hands search over the covers, like someone blind might frantically read Braille. In the dark, my eyes are looking but they see nothing. It is pitch black. I taste rubber band. I hear something. A kitten mewing? My throat vibrates. My chest hurts. I awaken with one hand at my neck and the other at my heart.

Date: Saturday, November 9

Topic: Damaged

Category: Feelings

Author: Ardenia Dovie Carroll

Location: 727 Rt. 323, Penny Pass, AR

Bruised bananas sell for less. Out of date bread does, too. Damaged things are worth less. The same with people. By <u>regular</u> standards. Some men aren't interested in women who haven't kept themselves pure. Jesus was different. The very people that most people judged as bad or distasteful were plenty good for Him. The ones that had been cast away, he welcomed with open arms. A warm smile. The unclean were greeted like brothers and sisters. When <u>He</u> looks, all He sees is what's real, and sincere, and what's possible by being whole. His love cancels out damage.

Date: Sunday, November 10

Topic: Still, Small Voice

Category: Action

Author: Ardenia Dovie Carroll

Location: 727 Rt. 323, Penny Pass, AR

If God talks in thunder, you are likely to notice. When God talks in a still, small voice, if you are not being quiet and attentive, you might miss Him. Some preachers stress the importance of praying every day. Dad agrees but he also says after you talk a little (out loud or with silent words) you need to just get still and wait a bit. He says that being quiet and listening is every bit as important as talking to God. That sometimes, for all the racket of our words, God can't get a word in edgewise. Sometimes I skip the prayer part and just listen.

Date: Monday, November 11

Topic: Sounds of Rain

Category: Action

Author: Ardenia Dovie Carroll

Location: 727 Rt. 323, Penny Pass, AR

Rain can sound startlingly different. The sound depends on what it's hitting. This means more than what I know it to mean - there's a life lesson in there somewhere.

Rain on our roof is different than on the church roof. There's the distinct sound of rain on a tin roof. On top of the bus. Car. While waiting under a leafy tree. On a dirt road. On pavement, umbrella, skin, wood. Rain on ice, rain on snow, rain on garden, rain on pond, rain on river.

Date: Tuesday, November 12

Topic: 2 Samuel 12, King James Version

Category: Poetry - Accidental

Author: Ardenia Dovie Carroll

Location: 727 Rt. 323, Penny Pass, AR

And anger was greatly kindled:
The poor man had nothing
And lay all night upon the earth.
The rich had exceeding many
Precious stones.
Who can tell whether God
will be gracious?

Date: Wednesday, November 13

Topic: Holding My Breath

Category: Feeling

Author: Ardenia Dovie Carroll

Location: 727 Rt. 323, Penny Pass, AR

I've heard people refer to a particular feeling as "waiting for the other shoe to drop." I just keep finding myself holding my breath. Tight in my chest. Tight in my belly. I have to <u>remind</u> myself to breath. I know I'm not really not breathing. Breathing is automatic and that's a good thing. But, I'm not breathing well. I'm not relaxing. When I catch myself tense, I have to walk myself through a process of loosening and spreading out. Have to shake the tingling from my fingers. Move some air from my nose to my naval. Have to remember God is with me.

Date: Thursday, November 14

Topic: In the Cradle of Your Lap

Category: Poetry – Intentional

Author: Ardenia Dovie Carroll

Location: 727 Rt. 323, Penny Pass, AR

Rock my body, rock my soul.
Like a mama, rock and roll
me, little itty-bitty me,
in the cradle of Your lap.
Let me sink and rest and dream.
Listening to creaks and to the cream
Of the chair, of Your voice
In the cradle of Your lap.

Date: Friday, November 15

Topic: Scared?

Category: Feeling

Author: Ardenia Dovie Carroll

Location: 727 Rt. 323, Penny Pass, AR

Maybe I'm just scared. I was so sick. All of a sudden. Out of nowhere. What if that happens again? What if that happens every time I have my period? Or even some of the time? I know that trusting God and trusting that He holds the future is supposed to make me feel better. And, it does for a second or two. Then, I'm back to being worried. Or scared. Feeling like life is too big for me. Too, too big to figure out. And, too big to not try to figure out. Then I feel so tired. On top of feeling scared and worried.

Date: Saturday, November 16

Topic:

Category:

Author: Ardenia Dovie Carroll

Location: 727 Rt. 323, Penny Pass, AR

Date: Sunday, November 17

Topic:

Category:

Author: Ardenia Dovie Carroll

Location: 727 Rt. 323, Penny Pass, AR

Date: Monday, November 18

Topic:

Category:

Author: Ardenia Dovie Carroll

Location: 727 Rt. 323, Penny Pass, AR

Date: Tuesday, November 19

Topic: The Quiet Game

Category: Thing

Author: Ardenia Dovie Carroll

Location: 727 Rt. 323, Penny Pass, AR

If you need or want little kids to get and stay
quiet, you can play a game. Say "Let's play The
Quiet Game!" in an excited voice. "We'll all get
quiet and see who can stay quiet the longest.
Now, remember, whoever talks first . . . loses."
Say "loses" like it's the worst thing in the world.
This will buy you at least a minute to catch your
breath or unravel your thoughts. Like an extended
time out, I've decided to just play the quiet game
for a while. Since Friday night. It hasn't even been
hard. I just don't feel like talking. I wish I could
figure out how to play the quiet brain game, too.

Date: Wednesday, November 20

Topic: God

Category: Person, Place

Author: Ardenia Dovie Carroll

Location: 727 Rt. 323, Penny Pass, AR

I <u>have</u> to speak in school, and to Mom and Dad, and at church. But I've been quiet the rest of the time, and I've figured out something. The one I don't want to talk to the most is God. I know. That's not good. We're to take everything to God. We are supposed to want to. But I don't. There's a part of me that thinks He's not been listening, anyway. I speculate, just like with little kids, the quiet game will get to be too much for me, and I'll hanker to open my mouth to Him and I'll inch my way back to His throne. And I suspect, He will be waiting. But will He really hear?

Date: Thursday, November 21

Topic: Dove

Category: Poetry – Intentional

Author: Ardenia Dovie Carroll

Location: 727 Rt. 323, Penny Pass, AR

Let me fall
At Your feet
And when I do
Prepare to meet
Me with love
With so much love
That I rise up
A healed, bright dove.

Date: Friday, November 22

Topic: The Rock-a-thon

Category: Thing

Author: Ardenia Dovie Carroll

Location: 727 Rt. 323, Penny Pass, AR

It's our youth group fundraiser. Sponsors pledge money for every hour we rock. We haul our rocking chairs to the fellowship hall. Wooden, creaky chairs as well as soft padded grandma rockers. It begins at 7pm and goes 'til 7am, when the donuts arrive. We rock all night long. Most are willing to trade rockers throughout the night so another part of our body can grow numb. The only breaks are staggered bathroom breaks. A few grownups supervise us. They talk quietly all night long; their constant hum makes it hard to stay awake. I have to be awake to rock; have to talk to stay awake.

Date: Saturday, November 23

Topic: Sleep

Category: Action

Author: Ardenia Dovie Carroll

Location: 727 Rt. 323, Penny Pass, AR

I SLEPT ALL DAY.

Date: Sunday, November 24

Topic: I Must Tell Jesus, Hymn # 179

Category: Action

Author: Ardenia Dovie Carroll

Location: 727 Rt. 323, Penny Pass, AR

"I must tell Jesus all of my troubles
I cannot bear my burdens alone
In my distress He kindly will help me
He ever loves and cares for his own.

     I must tell Jesus, I must tell Jesus
     I cannot bear my burdens alone
     I must tell Jesus, I must tell Jesus
     Jesus can help me, Jesus alone.

Tempted and tried I need a great Savior
One who can help my burdens to bear
I must tell Jesus, I must tell Jesus
He all my cares and sorrows will share."

Date: Monday, November 25

Topic: My Nest

Category: Thing

Author: Ardenia Dovie Carroll

Location: 727 Rt. 323, Penny Pass, AR

In the only other house I've ever lived in, there was a closet that ran down the entire length of the hall. Mama kept extra blankets on the second shelf. Before I could talk, I'd fidget my fingers in the crack between the sliding door and frame, and push it open. I'd put my knee on the first shelf and pull up, and do the same on the next shelf. Once on the blankets, I'd push the door until it was nearly closed. That shelf was waist high to Mom. I'd listen to her humming. And her footsteps. I'd peek as she walked by. Safe and all cozy, I'd burrow in like a bunny and sleep like a fawn.

Date: Tuesday, November 26

Topic: Trust

Category: Thing

Author: Ardenia Dovie Carroll

Location: 727 Rt. 323, Penny Pass, AR

I believe in Jesus and I trust Him. I believe the world is round and I can trust that it is because it is. What's the difference between believe and trust? Both are verbs. Both require something of me. Believe feels personal. Trust feels bigger. I can believe I'll make an A on my next test but I trust, even if I don't, it will be ok. I believe in angels; I trust God's around me one way or another, with or without angels. Both seem to ask something specific of me. I, my own self, put a little or a lot of effort into believing but I rest or surrender more in trusting.

Date: Wednesday, November 27

Topic: Preparation

Category: Action

Author: Ardenia Dovie Carroll

Location: 727 Rt. 323, Penny Pass, AR

We're on Thanksgiving break. Mama has already baked pumpkin and pecan pies. Since I like neither, I baked a whacky cake when I got home. She's got the alarm set for earlier than usual tomorrow morning. To get the turkey in. She asked if I wanted to get up, and watch, and learn. I said I thought I'd wait 'til I'm 14. But, I just now decided to set my own alarm and surprise her. I can see her face now. She'll be so happy. We'll work to get all of the regulars on the table at 2. By 3:30, the turkey will be off the carcass, leftovers will be in the frig and we'll all be dozing.

Date: Thursday, November 28

Topic: Thanksgiving

Category: Feeling

Author: Ardenia Dovie Carroll

Location: 727 Rt. 323, Penny Pass, AR

Mama's turkey and dressing were great. So was the ham. We stuffed ourselves. Daddy sprawled out on the couch. Mama headed to their bed. I needed to walk in crunchy leaves. The sky was solid blue. Zeke walked up. He surprised me. My eyes filled with tears. I don't know why. I tried to hide them but he took my arm and leaned down to look in my eyes. I shook my head. "It's hard. I don't even know what I want, but being with you and not being with you is hard. Sometimes I just want to go back to July." He put one arm around me and drew me to him. This is what I'm thankful for.

Date: Friday, November 29

Topic: Sharing Thanksgiving

Category: Thing, Action, Place

Author: Ardenia Dovie Carroll

Location: 727 Rt. 323, Penny Pass, AR

We have a big potluck at church on Friday after Thanksgiving. It's an annual meal, from 4 to 7 pm, for anyone and everyone. We announce it on the radio. Rather than wondering about the cleanliness of strangers' food preparation, we provide the entire meal. It's work, especially after the day before, but everyone does it cheerfully. Often, it's the only Thanksgiving food people get. This year, we had 6 turkeys, 7 hams, 5 tables of side dishes, and 3 dessert tables. Counting ourselves (we take turns sitting down and eating a little with our guests), we fed 153. 153 people giving thanks.

Date: Saturday, November 30

Topic: Song

Category: Feelings

Author: Ardenia Dovie Carroll

Location: 727 Rt. 323, Penny Pass, AR

Songs that aren't religious sometimes surprise me. They reach in and grab my stomach by its throat. And then, after that, whenever I hear those songs again, the same thing happens. The feeling? Alive, <u>and</u> something kin to longing. Belonging and being Longing at the same time. Sorrow and Surrender. Along with Too Much and Not Enough. All at once. Gospel songs sometimes touch me but not like this. This, it feels like prayer and pain and peace and purpose and plenty and power. James Taylor songs do this to me. Like his Long Ago and Far away. Carolina in My Mind. Fire and Rain. And, Hymn.

December

1974

Date: Sunday, December 1

Topic: The Question

Category: Thing, Action

Author: Ardenia Dovie Carroll

Location: 727 Rt. 323, Penny Pass, AR

After church tonight, I sat on the porch. I kept thinking there was something I was forgetting and if I got still enough, I'd remember what it was. I never did remember. And, even though I was bundled up, out in that cold I felt as exposed as the black naked trees. The wind wound around them and around me like a river wraps around boulders. A constant, troubling wearing and tearing away. Suddenly, I thought, "But what will be left?" No answer. But the question felt honest. And with it, I felt a flicker within. Of vim and vigor. A blink, a wink, a link, a brink.

Date: Monday, December 2

Topic: Listening

Category: Poetry - Intentional

Author: Ardenia Dovie Carroll

Location: 727 Rt. 323, Penny Pass, AR

I listen to what people say and
what they don't say.
I listen to the world. All of it,
every branch, every breeze, every stone,
every star.
I listen to my inner world - my words,
my thoughts,
my body, my skin,
my hands,
my heart.
Listening is anything but passive -
It takes perfect pitch.

Date: Tuesday, December 3

Topic: Flying

Category: Action

Author: Ardenia Dovie Carroll

Location: 727 Rt. 323, Penny Pass, AR

Last night I dreamt of flying. First, I was flying from one corner of my bedroom ceiling to the opposite. As I flew, the room got bigger. It grew to a church, then an old hay barn, a wide circus tent, an enclosed baseball field, a jungle, and finally to something that had no ceiling at all. Back and forth I traversed on an invisible line until, at last, in the end, I was flying untethered wherever my heart and wings and legs desired. Up and around, climbing and plunging and sweeping the air with my presence. The space in which I flew and I were greeting each other like long lost friends.

Date: Wednesday, December 4

Topic:

Category:

Author: Ardenia Dovie Carroll

Location: 727 Rt. 323, Penny Pass, AR

Date: Thursday, December 5

Topic: Miscarriage

Category: Thing, Action

Author: Ardenia Dovie Carroll

Location: 727 Rt. 323, Penny Pass, AR

Today, I asked Mama what losing Collie Jr. was like. First, she answered, "Sad. It was sad." I told her, "No, what was IT like?" She said she didn't want to scare me. I said it wouldn't. She said there was a lot of blood, and her cramps were something fierce, making her double over. She talked very slowly, and her eyes never left mine, and I didn't look away from hers either. The upper curves of my eyeballs stung from air. My stomach clenched. Then my heart shattered and when I blurted out, "Oh, Mama!" I was crying and then I was wailing. Mama's gentle voice said, "Tell me, Ardenia, tell me."

Date: Thursday, December 5

Topic: Truth

Category: Feelings

Author: Ardenia Dovie Carroll

Location: 727 Rt. 323, Penny Pass, AR

So I did. I told her about the camper and the pinch on the back of my arm and that he grabbed my breast and the ice on the floor and how I didn't like him at all and about his nasty words and waking with him outside the window and how afraid I was and how I wanted to be good and kind and how I didn't want to go get that recipe for her and how he slammed me against the counter and his private part was hard and his breathing was so hot and how his yucky wet hand hurt me inside and how I bled and how I've felt different ever since and how I'm sorry. How I'm so sorry.

Date: Thursday, December 5

Topic: Mama

Category: People, Action

Author: Ardenia Dovie Carroll

Location: 727 Rt. 323, Penny Pass, AR

Mama is a good listener. While I talked, she never said a single word. I was talking so fast, she couldn't have anyway. Tears ran down her face as fast as tears ran down mine. Her face changed many times. Every expression was a muddled puddle of Love and something else. I think I saw Confusion, Alertness, Figuring Out, Comprehension, Alarm, and Pain. And Love, always Love. Only when my words finally stopped coming did she draw me to her. She pulled me onto her lap like I was little bitty. Only then was her crying out loud like mine. Only then did she call out, "Colle, Collie, Collie!"

Date: Thursday, December 5

Topic: We Three

Category: People, Action

Author: Ardenia Dovie Carroll

Location: 727 Rt. 323, Penny Pass, AR

We heard Daddy before we saw him. He was running through the house. When he opened up the bedroom door, he was ready for almost anything. I cried, "Daddy, I'm sorry." He looked around for the emergency. As if looking for fire. Or blood. Puzzled, he looked from me to Mama. Mama said to me "Shhh," and to Daddy, "Sit down, Daddy. Ardenia has told me something very upsetting and it's going to upset you, too. You need to listen from beginning to end, Collie. We'll put the pieces together a little bit later. But for now, you just listen, ok?" Daddy nodded. And he sat down on my other side.

Date: Thursday, December 5

Topic: Daddy

Category: People, Action

Author: Ardenia Dovie Carroll

Location: 727 Rt. 323, Penny Pass, AR

Because I couldn't tell it to Daddy, I just couldn't, Mama told it all using the same words I used (like private part instead of penis). I couldn't look at him, either. I just looked at my knees. I've never felt my daddy be so still. It wasn't a stillness that echoes absence; it was a stillness that's full of presence. Mama had to stop a few times and take a breath. Daddy's breath was quivery. When she finished there was only the sound of our sadness and then I felt Daddy's wide warm hand span most of my back. "Oh, Sugar," he said and then I was in his lap.

Date: Friday, December 6

Topic: Family

Category: People, Thing

Author: Ardenia Dovie Carroll

Location: 727 Rt. 323, Penny Pass, AR

Last night, after we were tired from crying, Mama ran me a hot bath and gave me two Tylenol. While I soaked, their voices rolled back and forth in the living room. I think I heard Daddy say, "God, damn it," but he was crying so I can't be sure. When I crawled into bed, Mama snuggled behind me, Daddy sat on the edge of the bed. He said, "Sugar, we are sorry he did this to you, and that you've been shouldering it all by yourself. We love you so much, Ardenia." He nodded over and over. Like he didn't know what else he could say. Then, "You get some sleep tonight. Tomorrow's a new day, Sugar."

Date: Friday, December 6

Topic: Today

Category: Action

Author: Ardenia Dovie Carroll

Location: 727 Rt. 323, Penny Pass, AR

And today <u>is</u> a new day. All of our eyes are swollen. But I feel lighter than I've felt since before the revival. I stayed home from school. At breakfast, Daddy said he had a few ideas about next steps, but since it had happened to me and I'd had more time to think about it all, he was wondering what I thought. I told him I'd imagined a lot of unchristian-like things. He said he had, too, and glanced at Mama. Setting down her juice glass, Mama murmured, "It's easy for us to think of all kinds of things to do that young man. We must ask God to help us know what's best."

Date: Friday, December 6

Topic: Dead Center

Category: Place

Author: Ardenia Dovie Carroll

Location: 727 Rt. 323, Penny Pass, AR

Daddy told me I might remember more and if I do, I should tell Mama or him. No matter what it is. I asked him to walk over to the church with me. We sat on a pew in the dead center. I told him I hadn't known what to do. I was trying to be good. I told him I'd kept praying and asking for help but the help I was asking for didn't come. I was un. pre. pared. I didn't know what to do. Daddy said, "You're my girl, Ardenia, you can come to <u>me</u>." And then, go figure, we started crying again. After a bit, he took his hankie and wiped my tears first, wiped his, and held my hand in both of his.

Date: Saturday, December 7

Topic: Confrontation

Category: Action

Author: Ardenia Dovie Carroll

Location: 727 Rt. 323, Penny Pass, AR

We had a family meeting: Daddy's going to meet with Brother Bryar and Asshole. (He says it's just fine if I want to call him that for now.) Mama doesn't want him going alone. I don't want anyone from our church to know. Daddy says the Presbyter has to know so he's going to tell him and ask him to go along. Mama says that young man must be stopped. Daddy said he could make sure it never happens again. Mama said that's the last thing we need. I said I'm not so sure. She changed the subject: She's made a doctor's appointment for me in the next county. Week after next.

Date: Sunday, December 8

Topic: Strawberries

Category:

Author: Ardenia Dovie Carroll

Location: 727 Rt. 323, Penny Pass, AR

This afternoon, we had another family meeting. I think it was planned. Daddy and I were in the living room when Mama carried in a tray with bowls of summer strawberries she'd frozen for winter. She handed out the bowls and said, "Ardenia, we still have some questions" at which I nearly shouted, "<u>Tell me!</u> <u>None</u> of it makes any sense because I <u>couldn't</u> have been pregnant because my private parts have <u>never</u> fit with a boy's private parts. Except miracles <u>do</u> happen. Like the virgin Mary and baby Jesus." They looked at each other. Daddy took a big breath and set down his bowl.

Date: Sunday, December 8

Topic: Unbelievable

Category:

Author: Ardenia Dovie Carroll

Location: 727 Rt. 323, Penny Pass, AR

I scooped Mama's sweet strawberries into my mouth and continued. "That's the only thing I can come up with. It was a bad miracle instead of a good one. Unbelievable, I know, but it happened just the same." Daddy looked at Mama who said, "Well, we think it's explainable. We've been wondering how his hand got wet." Without looking at Daddy, I told how white goo came out of his private part and he put his hand in it. Well, let's just say Sex Ed left out a lot. The sperm <u>can</u> reach the egg in more ways than one. That night I must have gotten pregnant!

Date: Sunday, December 8

Topic: Anger

Category: Feeling

Author: Ardenia Dovie Carroll

Location: 727 Rt. 323, Penny Pass, AR

I told Daddy I don't want to know what happens to Asshole but I hope it's really bad, awful in fact, whatever it is. And lucky for him it's not up to me. Daddy asked me if I'd like to go a few rounds with him. I said, "Yeah, with him tied up and me with a cast iron skillet in my hand." Daddy patted my shoulder "He'll get his, Ardenia. Believe you me, he'll get his. You have a right to rage. Who knows, one day, you might find that rage is more a fume. Later on, that fume might be more an ember, and one day that ember might go out for good. For good, Ardenia. Somehow for good.

Date: Monday, December 9

Topic: My Parts

Category: Feelings

Author: Ardenia Dovie Carroll

Location: 727 Rt. 323, Penny Pass, AR

One part of me feels like crying, another part feels like laughing. One part finally feels smart, while another feels stupid and ignorant. One part feels heavy with knowledge, another part feels lighter from the same knowledge. One part asks, "Did this really happen" while another part answers, "It most certainly did." One part feels relief, one part feels ready to move on, yet another part asks how? One part feels like I've finished a marathon, another like one's just beginning. One part feels dirty and tired, but a bigger part feels clear and honest and loved.

Date: Tuesday, December 10

Topic: ~~Cherished~~ Balance

Category: Feeling

Author: Ardenia Dovie Carroll

Location: 727 Rt. 323, Penny Pass, AR

If you're cherished, someone considers you to be precious, irreplaceable. Beloved. It's the exact opposite of abandoned, despised, forsaken. I know God cherishes me. Jesus does, of course. And I'm 100% sure Mama and Daddy do. But if all that "knowing" was placed on one side of a balance scale and the "feeling" of being cherished on the other, they would not be equal. Right now, even with all the "knowing" in my head, the "feeling" in my heart just isn't there. I wish I could wave a magic wand and level out the two sides.

Date: Wednesday, December 11

Topic: Miracle

Category:

Author: Ardenia Dovie Carroll

Location: 727 Rt. 323, Penny Pass, AR

It's December. Nearly Christmas. Jesus came to save us from sin and he came to us as a baby through a miracle birth. This year feels different, with all that's happened to me. I told Daddy today that I'm not at all sorry or sad I miscarried. That as precious as babies are, I don't want that one. That maybe losing the baby was my miracle. He agreed with his nodding. I told him how I'd just kept trying to figure it out and couldn't. He said, "Well, Sugar, there was a lot to figure out." Then he reached out and took my hand and we listened to the secondhand tick time on his wrist.

Date: Thursday, December 12

Topic: Show Me

Category: Feelings

Author: Ardenia Dovie Carroll

Location: 727 Rt. 323, Penny Pass, AR

Mama used to ask me to make different kinds of faces. Happy. Sad. Angry. Puzzled. Surprised with eyes and mouth in 3 big "O's." Tonight, we sat in the living room. All thinking our own thoughts. I felt her looking at me. She asked, "What kind of face is that?" I told her I wasn't sure. "Maybe a lot of them rolled into one?" She said, "Life is that way sometimes. As soon as we can name one feeling, there's another to name." She got up and came to sit next to me, and all three of us took turns sighing. Then it just got funny. So we giggled. But at the end of giggling were more sighs.

Date: Friday, December 13

Topic: Cozy

Category: Feeling

Author: Ardenia Dovie Carroll

Location: 727 Rt. 323, Penny Pass, AR

It's so cold outside. Hard to get warm and stay warm. The heater is blazing but we've all chosen quilts to keep handy. I have Touching Stars. All of the stars' centers are yellow but only three of the outsides have a match. All of the rest are of different fabrics. I can sit and look at this quilt for hours. I do and I have. On his lap, Daddy has a heavy one made out of polyester that no one knows the name of. Mama has finished her Sunny Lane and is using it but very carefully. She's placed a tea towel in her lap to rest her cup on. We are cozy tonight.

Date: Saturday, December 14

Topic: Beauty

Category: Thing, Feeling, Action

Author: Ardenia Dovie Carroll

Location: 727 Rt. 323, Penny Pass, AR

Beauty is as beauty does. I've heard it all my life. Mama reminds me of this when I'm acting ugly or could be acting better. More than once, she's told the story of how, when she was very little, there was a gift exchange and one girl only had a hand-stitched handkerchief to give. When the girl she'd given it to opened it up, she'd wrinkled her nose and the giver's feelings were so hurt. Once I asked Mama, "Were you one of those girls?" I'll never forget, she smiled sadly and said, "I've been both, Ardenia. And so have you." So the take-away is Beauty is Love. And love is always beautiful.

Date: Sunday, December 15

Topic: Depths of Love

Category: Feeling

Author: Ardenia Dovie Carroll

Location: 727 Rt. 323, Penny Pass, AR

"A wonderful Savior is Jesus my Lord,
          He taketh my burden away;
He holdeth me up and I shall not be moved,
          He giveth me strength as my day.
He hideth my soul in the cleft of the rock
          That shadows a dry, thirsty land;
He hideth my life in the depths of His love,
          And covers me there with His hand,
And covers me there with His hand.
          He hideth my life in the depths of His love,
And covers me there with His hand.
          And covers me there with His hand."

Date: Monday, December 16

Topic: The Exam

Category: Thing

Author: Ardenia Dovie Carroll

Location: 727 Rt. 323, Penny Pass, AR

Take off panties, lay down on a high noisy paper-covered exam table. Scoot your bottom to the very edge. Until it hangs off a bit. Put your heels in cold stirrups. Spread apart your knees. The doctor sits with his face at your private area and looks. He picks up a shiny speculum, puts on an embarrassing squeeze of clear jelly. Tells you to relax. Impossible. He slides it inside of you. Cold. Hurts. Tears fill eyes. You can feel it open. He swabs with long q-tips. Takes the speculum out and reaches inside of you to feel around. It hurts. He never looks straight at your face. It's over.

Date: Tuesday, December 17

Topic: Song

Category: Thing, Feeling

Author: Ardenia Dovie Carroll

Location: 727 Rt. 323, Penny Pass, AR

I've thought about the exam again and again. It's the only time other than during the Revival that something touched and went into my vagina. It hurt but Mama held my hand. It was embarrassing, my naked bottom. Mama held my hand. During the exam, I kept thinking "my body is supposed to be covered". I kept telling myself, "This is a good thing" and "Now I can stop worrying about my insides" and "That pain had nothing to do with a period." I kept looking at Mama, who loved me with her eyes. After the exam and now today, in my mind, I keep saying, hearing, "I'm ok. I'm ok. I'm ok!"

Date: Wednesday, December 18

Topic: Alarm

Category: Feeling

Author: Ardenia Dovie Carroll

Location: 727 Rt. 323, Penny Pass, AR

I hate thinking about that night, and I hate to think about Daddy and Mama thinking about that night. I wonder how things, _if_ things, would have been different had I been different. It's not like I did something wrong but I made some mistakes and I've learned some lessons. Mama and Daddy say they have, too. The biggest thing: If ever again I have that unmistakable feeling I felt when I first met him, I won't push it away. I will let it be what it really is. An alarm of adrenalin clanging and screaming and ringing with truth and warning and love. I will pay attention! I will tell. I'll ask for help.

Date: Thursday, December 19

Topic: Ready, Set, Go.

Category: Feeling

Author: Ardenia Dovie Carroll

Location: 727 Rt. 323, Penny Pass, AR

My smoothing, soothing, sustaining song has been singing to me steadily. Sunrise, Sunset. "I'm ok. I'm really ok." Everything within me responds with a "Thank You!" that is as lidless as the nighttime sky; as sincere as star splendor. I am feeling restored. Understood. Relieved, alive. Ready to live. Because Hope is here. I hold hope like a baby bird is held in one's hand. Had I known how telling would have healed me, I would have told right away. That very first afternoon. May shame and ignorance never silence me again.

Date: Friday, December 20

Topic: My Heart

Category: People

Author: Ardenia Dovie Carroll

Location: 727 Rt. 323, Penny Pass, AR

Sometimes my heart feels like an instrument that is being played. Or waiting to be played. By the whole world. Or by God. Like my "real" chest was created all hollowed out, all ready to vibrate with sound and experience and beauty and love. Sometimes I feel something quick and remarkable and clean and clear and absolutely pure deep inside of my heart and when I do, there's the sudden thought, "Oh! Here's the real me" and then it's gone, all but for the memory and a homesickness for more.

Date: Saturday, December 21

Topic: Winter Slippers!

Category: Thing

Author: Ardenia Dovie Carroll

Location: 727 Rt. 323, Penny Pass, AR

I am so excited about giving Mama and Daddy their new slippers. More even than seeing what they give me for Christmas! It took some conniving. They never leave their old things out anywhere. I slipped into their closet to write down their sizes but the tags were either missing or the writing had worn off. So I had to slip out and back in again and trace them with paper and pencil! It took two pieces of paper taped together for Daddy's. Then, I carefully folded and saved them. When I went shopping, the salesman asked what size, I unfolded and said "Walla!"

Date: Sunday, December 22

Topic: We Wish You a Merry Christmas

Category: Place

Author: Ardenia Dovie Carroll

Location: 727 Rt. 323, Penny Pass, AR

Between both services, we managed to work in
Away in a Manger, Silent Night, The First Noel,
Hark! The Herald Angels Sing, It Came Upon a Mid-
night Clear, Joy to the World, O Come All Ye
Faithful, and O Little Town of Bethlehem. Tonight,
when Daddy asked for requests, a little boy piped
up and asked for "We Wish You a Merry Christmas." It isn't in the hymnal but Dad said we'd
close with that. Before he dismissed us, he told
us to mill around and sing while we looked at each
other. So we milled and smiled and shook hands and
hugged and sang that one verse about 20 times.

Date: Monday, December 23

Topic: Outhouse

Category: Place

Author: Ardenia Dovie Carroll

Location: 727 Rt. 323, Penny Pass, AR

If I could bet, I'd bet that we're going to have a white Christmas. It will be beautiful and perfect. As long as our pipes don't freeze. Unbeknownst to many, outhouses are still used in 1974. In AR, in Penny Pass, at Olive Branch Assembly of God Church, and if our well runs dry or the pipes freeze, Mom, Dad, and I have to use them. In Summer, we face snakes, endless spiders, and the gagging smell. In Winter, we shiver up the hill bundled up like the Michelin man, try to uncover just our privates and hover over the seat: it's too cold to touch. We can barely relax to pee, let alone poop.

Date: Tuesday, December 24

Topic: O Holy Night

Category: Place

Author: Ardenia Dovie Carroll

Location: 727 Rt. 323, Penny Pass, AR

Joseph led Mary to a stable. Animals shuffled, making room. Angels held their breath for the world. Mary's body tightened and pressed and opened until baby Jesus was born. Then, angels burst into song and I think every star shone brighter that night. Who on earth could have known just how one small baby would make such a difference? Gentle Loving Teacher, Savior Dying on the Cross, but this night, this holy night, we again behold and fall in love with a hungry baby. A little one with the tiniest of toes and fingers, and eyes that pierced the world with love.

Date: Wednesday, December 25

Topic: This Morning, Christmas Morning

Category: Place

Author: Ardenia Dovie Carroll

Location: 727 Rt. 323, Penny Pass, AR

I could hardly stand it! I woke up first, of course! I'm the kid! I plugged in the lights and put their gifts in the very front. They got up, walked through the living room, noticed the new presents, and smiled. Daddy made coffee; Mom and I, cocoa. I announced, "Well, looks like Santa came." I told them to open them at the same time. But Mama began very slowly. Daddy grinned, bent down to slide out of his old slippers into his new. I looked at Mama, but she'd stopped opening to wipe tears. "Go ahead, Mama, you're going to like them." She said, "I love them" before she ever opened the box.

Date: Wednesday, December 25

Topic: Presents

Category: Things

Author: Ardenia Dovie Carroll

Location: 727 Rt. 323, Penny Pass, AR

These new slippers. Especially Mama's. It's like they are golden. Mama keeps admiring hers from one side, then the other, stretching out one foot at a time. "Ardenia, they are lovely." "So <u>comfortable</u>." "Like little <u>pillows</u> for my feet," and "What a nice surprise!" They chuckled when I told the story of how I traced Daddy's old ones to get the right size. Daddy wondered how old his old ones were. Neither could remember. My big present came in a tiny box. A necklace. Silver. One white pearl clings to the slender chain and one tiny diamond clings to the pearl. It's beautiful.

Date: Wednesday, December 25

Topic: My Christmas Content

Category: Place, Feeling

Author: Ardenia Dovie Carroll

Location: 727 Rt. 323, Penny Pass, AR

Content is more of a place than a feeling. It's a place where everything is A-O-K. Where a person feels relaxed and momentarily satisfied. The place where <u>not one more thing</u> is needed. Nor wanted. You don't feel bubbly inside with happiness; you feel calm and settled. All is well. It is well. With my soul. And my heart, and brain, and body, and God, and who I am, and who I will be. For a moment, or several minutes, it's feeling the fullness and beauty and grace and rightness of your life. That you're in accord. And right where you are supposed to be.

Date: Thursday, December 26

Topic: Telling Someone Else

Category: Action

Author: Ardenia Dovie Carroll

Location: 727 Rt. 323, Penny Pass, AR

Mama and Daddy said it isn't necessary to tell anyone else. They said it might be <u>best</u> not to. But Zeke came over this afternoon. When he asked, "What happened, Ardenia? Really, what happened?" I took a big breath and said, "You won't believe it." He said, "I'd believe anything you tell me." I said, "First, I might have loved you. I still might." He blinked and waited. Then, I told an abbreviated version: "The teenage son of the Revival preacher nearly raped me one night. He scared me real bad first. He's an asshole." I waited. "It gets worse but that's probably enough." He asked, "Worse? How?"

Date: Thursday, December 26

Topic: More Telling

Category: Action

Author: Ardenia Dovie Carroll

Location: 727 Rt. 323, Penny Pass, AR

We were freezing. Sitting on the front porch pew, scarfs wrapped around our necks. He wore a stocking cap, I had on gloves, he had his hands in his pockets. I told him I didn't think I could tell him any more. That it might change the way he thought of me and I didn't know if I could stand any more of that. We sat and shivered. Then, he said the same thing, "Worse than that? Ardenia, how?" "I can't tell you the details. But he hurt me. And in a way you wouldn't even believe, I ended up pregnant but I didn't even know it, Zeke. I didn't know it." He looked up at the sky, "Then what?"

Date: Thursday, December 26

Topic: And More

Category: Action

Author: Ardenia Dovie Carroll

Location: 727 Rt. 323, Penny Pass, AR

"Then I miscarried, but, get this, I didn't know that either. That's how stupid I was, Zeke. It hurt so <u>bad</u>. I kept trying to figure out what was happening but I couldn't. It was like Mr. Griffin's complicated math word problems, but without all of the information you need to solve it. And you don't even know what's missing." Zeke whispered, "Jesus," and pulled me to him. I laid my head on his shoulder. "Then what?" "After all that, I told Mom and Dad. I had to go see a doctor. Dad wanted to kill the asshole just like I did; Mama wouldn't let him. The last thing we need is Dad in jail."

Date: Thursday, December 26

Topic: Now

Category: Feeling

Author: Ardenia Dovie Carroll

Location: 727 Rt. 323, Penny Pass, AR

"Then what?" "Well, that part just happened a few weeks ago, Zeke." We sat there, freezing cold but for one solid warm streak where my right side and his left side pressed together. He said he didn't know what to say. I asked him to keep it a secret because it's so embarrassing. He crossed his heart and hoped to die. I let him. Then he said, "It is hard to believe. I keep thinking, Really? All of that was happening? Every time I saw you, I knew something was wrong. It was all this. So much makes more sense now." After a while, he asked, "Are you ok, Ardenia?" I answered, "I'm better now."

Date: Friday, December 27

Topic: What I Know

Category: People

Author: Ardenia Dovie Carroll

Location: 727 Rt. 323, Penny Pass, AR

I know that people can be good, and kind. Gentle, yet firm. Open, yet with a serious do-not-cross-this line. I know people can be creative and generous and trusting and curious and brave. And more than one of these at a time. I know that people can be so beautiful that tears spring right up from the fountain of your heart. And now? Now I know that some people are mean. So mean and ugly that you can barely fathom it. So mean it must be evil. So great is their cruelty that you feel a double sorrow. The first from their heartlessness. The second from knowing it's possible.

Date: Saturday, December 28

Topic: The Top 100

Category: Thing

Author: Ardenia Dovie Carroll

Location: 727 Rt. 323, Penny Pass, AR

Today was the American Top 40 Year End Countdown. I listened to the whole thing. Out of the top 100 songs, I knew every word to 61 of them. I made a tally mark at the end of every song to keep count. I knew some of the words to most of the rest. When the songs I can't stand played, I knew I had three minutes to go to the bathroom, get food, grab clothes to fold, etc. The top four songs for 1974: Come and Get Your Love, Love's Theme, Seasons in the Sun, and The Way We Were. The sun's out; the snow has melted. Zeke and I waved from our porches today. Wearing silly grins.

Date: Sunday, December 29

Topic: Elephants and I's

Category: Thing

Author: Ardenia Dovie Carroll

Location: 727 Rt. 323, Penny Pass, AR

Last night I dreamed. There were two I's. (That's incorrect but "There were two me's" is all wrong. Dreams insist on being followed the way they occur.) So: I and another I were both riding beasts of burdens. Elephants. Buddy sat astride the Elephant named Agony. And Bliss was astride Adventure. Or was it the other way around? Was Agony carried along by the Elephant Buddy, and Elephant Bliss carried Adventure? I guess it doesn't really matter. The elephants and my I's were nearly inseparable. I can still feel the mountain of animal underneath me.

Date: Monday, December 30

Topic: Heartedness

Category: People

Author: Ardenia Dovie Carroll

Location: 727 Rt. 323, Penny Pass, AR

There's lionhearted, stouthearted, lighthearted, kind-hearted, tenderhearted, good hearted, warm hearted, cold hearted, hard hearted, mean hearted, brave hearted, weak hearted, halfhearted, single hearted, truehearted, bighearted, sad hearted, chicken hearted, high hearted, open hearted, wide hearted, and bro-kenhearted. The heart is the center, isn't it? The center from which we reach out to the world and everyone in it. The heart includes our feelings and what we believe about ourselves and others. Our heart deep down is our personal constitution. My heart - the kind of heart I have - is me.

Date: Tuesday, December 31

Topic: Quarterly Card Catalog Update

Category: Feeling

Author: Ardenia Dovie Carroll

Location: 727 Rt. 323, Penny Pass, AR

365 days; 393 filled out cards. One whole year of thoughts. I did it! And thank God I did. Thank _me_ I did. I always thought triumph was a public thing with others clapping and cheering and shouting your name as you cross the finish line. Silly me. Today I feel victorious. And not another person knows about this card catalog. This feeling is quiet but so big that my bones feel denser. This Dec 31? I feel stronger. My spirit feels true. My heart still ga-thumps with love. And now with Mama and Daddy by my side, my outlook looks out with hope. Hope. That might be all I really need.

January
1975

Date: Wednesday, January 1, 1975

Topic: Gardenia

Category: Thing

Author: Ardenia Dovie Carroll

Location: 727 Rt. 323, Penny Pass, AR

Had Mama loved Magnolia blossoms more than Gardenias, my name could have been Agnolia. Both flowers are beautiful and fragrant. Both are white petaled with yellow centers. Magnolia blossoms are as big as dinner plates. Gardenias are no bigger than a child's cheek and have thin petals. Tonight, after we finished the dishes, instead of dusting the top of her gardenia candle, Mama picked it up and found her little book of matches in a drawer. She lit it and we sat at the table and swallowed the scent of gardenia. Her lips touched my cheek as she whispered, "To you, Ardenia Dovie, to you."

Author's Note

Like Ardenia Dovie, I turned 13 in 1974. Like her, I was a preacher's kid in rural Arkansas and lived in a parsonage. Our back door was not more than 30 feet from the church's side door.

My childhood was filled with lots of love, lots of laughter, and lots of church. When I was about nine or ten years old, Daddy began pastoring rural churches; our family of five stayed in one place no longer than three years, and sometimes a scant 12 months. That may sound bleak, but we rang country church bells at 9 a.m. calling the entire community to church, we rode horses and dirt bikes, and bought penny candy at the old country store. We received tithes of live chickens, used outhouses, and built revival brush arbors by hand. We baptized in the Kings River. We ate Sunday dinner on the grounds. We were welcomed in everyone's homes. We learned to say hello with open hearts and to say goodbye with grateful hearts. And we told stories.

Truly, one of my greatest inheritances is an all-out love for story. Even before I could read well, I loved Bible stories. And I knew them well. I pretended to preach so that I could tell and re-tell them. I saw David's slingshot, I could feel the weight of it in my hand. I saw Moses' floating cradle, and became Miriam stirring not a bulrush. I felt the fire in Daniel's furnace, the floundering in Peter's faith, the incredulousness of Nicodemus's eyesight, the doubt in Thomas's mind, the sorrow of Mary at the crucifixion. I wasn't the least bit interested in trying to extrapolate *meanings*. Something happened in the telling of the stories and that, for me, was plenty.

Wherever we lived, we were always surrounded by loving, generous (and, yes, interesting!) people, but I regard the three years we lived in Batavia, Arkansas as being the best years of my childhood.

During that time, my favorite pastime was going to the church after school. Alone. Praying, thinking, singing, listening. As the late afternoon sunlight came through the windows and touched the quiet, I knew something beautiful and important was taking place within those walls: Stories. We weren't just telling ancient Bible stories that timelessly, limitlessly, rendered new interpretations, *we* were stories that were being written right then. All of our life stories were unfolding right before my very eyes.

I sat in certain spots on the worn benches and brought to mind the individuals that "claimed" them during the services. I thought about the events of their lives like chapter titles in books: failure, despair, destruction, remorse, hope, courage, determination, and triumph. I stood in front of the solid wooden pulpit and rubbed my hands across its slanted top. I rested my palms in the exact places where generations of ministers had rested theirs. And like they, as I stood there, I would recall the precious congregants, babes and elders, rich and poor, kind and still working on it, and felt my heart warm to each one. I felt honored to be a witness to their life stories and to be living out mine in their presence.

While my religious and spiritual views have changed steadily and significantly from those of my childhood, I cherish those conscious beginnings of my journey with The One Source. I carry these early experiences, and they continue to shape me.

Like Ardenia, I was always observing and always listening. I've been told that both come naturally to me. Chaplaincy and ministerial training fostered and honed those skills. Knowing how to listen with the totality of my being, being willing to be changed by what I hear, and honoring what I hear were all precursors to and the foundation for writing Ardenia's story. I never imagined that writing a book would be simply continuing to do what I do every day with clients: Listen. Pay attention. Listen. Take notes. Ponder. Listen.

Now, more about Ardenia Dovie's Card Catalog. All characters are fictitious. Plain and simple, Ardenia Dovie is not me or anyone else I've ever met. None of the other characters are actual people either. Except for Jude Power, most assume characteristics of people I love and respect. As for events, I like to say that Ardenia has borrowed some of my memories to tell her story. Some of what she writes about are composites of real occurrences from my life, ministry, and chaplaincy. Blending these preserves confidentiality.

Ardenia Dovie disclosed her name when she started whispering in my ear to tell her story. All other names – Collie Cade, Ruby, Shep, Zeke, and the Powers –were derived by googling "old Southern names." It felt as if I'd hit a bullseye when I happened upon each of their names. There is no Skiddy, Arkansas and Penny Pass is completely fabricated but I tasted copper in my mouth when that name bubbled up from somewhere.

This tale is purely Ardenia Dovie's. She and I share some coming-of-age perspectives and experiences but I wasn't raped when I was thirteen years old. (Once, though, as a young widow of only a few weeks, I narrowly escaped. I made it home with missing buttons, shredded pantyhose, and shaking legs. Hours later, I was still trying to slow my heartbeat and breath.)

Ardenia Dovie began to nudge me six months after my parents died just nine weeks apart. I scribbled notes during the day and slept with paper and pen so I could jot down catalog card topics and bits of content as soon as they came to me. When I began to actually write, I had no idea how her account would end. I only knew that her cards were written over the span of a year, and that she would be assaulted. I had a strong feeling she would be pregnant. There were moments when I couldn't conceive how I could capture what was unfolding in the space she and I shared. My mantra was "a few lines at a time, twelve short lines at a time." Her sexual assault, pregnancy, miscarriage, and finally telling her parents were incidents that were revealed to me just as they were to you, dear reader, one card at a time.

As I wrote her story, I reminisced my own 1974. I held and scrutinized family pictures, leafed through school yearbooks, ambled down rural roads past old homes, and remembered, remembered, remembered...all while working through the real tasks of grieving. That journeying was a healing balm and I thank Ardenia Dovie for it.

One final note. Some people have wondered why I wrote, or how I could have written, a book about the violation of a sweet child. My first answer is because Ardenia Dovie Carroll asked. I've not yet declined listening to anyone's hard, painful story and I wasn't about to start with her. Second, through Ardenia's experience, I hope to give tribute to the courage, resilience, hope, and the search for beauty, connection, meaning, and love that children who have been violated possess. The abuse, violence, rape, and even brutal deaths aren't ever the whole story. In this telling, I acknowledge the whole story.

About the Author

Jan Huneycutt Lightner grew up as a preacher's kid in the hills of Arkansas. She married young, mothered young, was widowed young, and grand-mothered young. She often draws from personal memories while writing, but the fictitious events in Ardenia Dovie's Card Catalog are clearly and only Ardenia's. This is Jan's first book. Some of the sources of inspiration for the book can be found on her website: author.janhuneycuttlightner.com. Feel free to connect with her there.

Jan is a clinically-trained chaplain, pastoral counselor, and grief counselor as well as an ordained interfaith/interspiritual minister. In her private practice, she provides emotional and spiritual support and grief counseling to individuals navigating the hardships that life inevitably brings. She also facilitates memorials and officiates weddings in the state of Arkansas. (janhuneycuttlightner.com)

She and her husband live in Bella Vista, Arkansas alongside deer, fox, squirrels, raccoons, chipmunks, owls, and hawks. Her deepest joy comes from connecting deeply with others. Her greatest teachers are the ones who happen to be sitting with her at any given moment. While her heart easily opens to everyone, it simply sings when she's with her kids and grandkids.

Jan contributes to a nonprofit that helps sexually abused children find their voice. Book sales help determine the gift amount.